These Deadly Words

Nichole Heydenburg

THESE DEADLY WORDS

Also by

Adult books:

The Long Shadow on the Stage- Book 1 in The Long Shadow Series

The Long Shadow of Memory- Book 2 in The Long Shadow Series

The Long Shadow of Death- Book 3 in The Long Shadow Series

Young adult books (standalones):

The Quiet Girl- Revenge thriller

These Deadly Words- Supernatural thriller

Don't Look Inside- Psychological thriller

Dead Girls Can't Smile- Psychological thriller

Content Warnings

swearing, alcoholism, underage drinking, mentions of suicide,
and murder

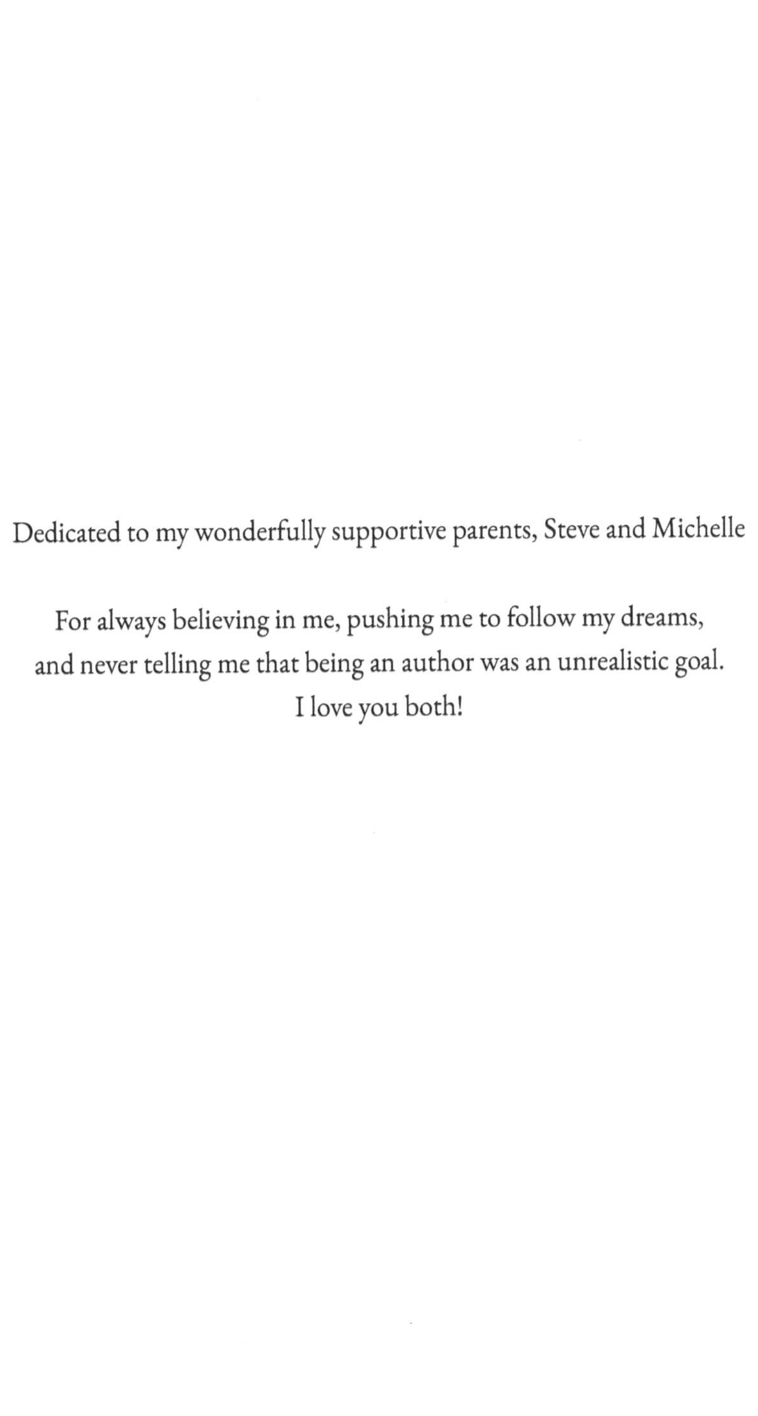

Dedicated to my wonderfully supportive parents, Steve and Michelle

For always believing in me, pushing me to follow my dreams,
and never telling me that being an author was an unrealistic goal.
I love you both!

Prologue

March 1988

Raindrops fell harshly against the umbrella, adding to the dreariness of the funeral. Leah squeezed her boyfriend's hand, huddling closer to him. Vincent gripped her hand, like he was holding on for dear life. And in a way, he was. The rain splashed around them as they stood in front of the casket being lowered into the ground.

The smooth mahogany was reflective in the rain. Leah wore the only suitable outfit that she had for a funeral—a simple black A-line dress her mom had bought her several years ago. She paired it with black flats, and a silk headband held back her normally untidy light brown bangs. Vincent looked handsome in a black dress shirt and slacks with his flowing chestnut-brown hair tied back into his usual ponytail.

Not many people had shown up at Vincent's dad's funeral. Leah had convinced her twin sister, Ava, to attend the service with Noah, Ava's boyfriend. A few of Vincent's dad's friends were there, and some of Leah's and Vincent's friends from school had shown up briefly. But everyone had left once it started downpouring. It was as if God himself was mourning the unfair death of a person who had been ripped from the earth too soon. Now it was only the two of them with the pastor and pallbearers.

With their high school graduation only a few weeks away, it was a terrible time for Vincent to lose his dad—not that any time would be easier. He was barely a legal adult, and now he had to find his way on his own.

As tears rolled down Vincent's face, he sniffled and turned his face away from Leah. She suspected he didn't want her to see him crying. This was the hardest thing they had gone through together. Leah didn't know how to handle Vincent's blatant suffering. His dad's suicide had shocked everyone who knew him, but Vincent most of all. Leah vowed to do whatever it took to help him through this terrible ordeal.

"I love you," she whispered to him.

Vincent only nodded in response.

All Leah wanted was to go back to the way things were before—when life was easy and carefree, and all they cared about was graduating from high school and going away to college. But something had irreparably changed in Vincent; she didn't think he would be the same person she had fallen in love with anymore. Losing a parent was bad enough, but to lose his dad to suicide when no one had suspected he was suffering was sure to change him.

Leah wanted to make things better. Maybe they could go on a road trip together. Vincent had always enjoyed camping and hiking with his dad. Maybe a trip together was what they needed to mend whatever was broken. Leah smiled and rested her head on Vincent's firm shoulder. Yes, a road trip would be perfect. It would fix everything.

Chapter 1: Leah

April 1988

The snowstorm bombarded the woods, leaving them trapped in the mountains of Asheville, unable to find their tent or their van. The harsh wind whipped around Leah, causing her silky brunette hair to swirl around her face, obscuring her view even further. Everywhere she turned her head, all she saw was glistening white. She held an arm in front of her face and braced herself against the howling wind, reaching out for Vincent with her other arm. His comforting hand found hers. Their fingers laced together as they had so many times over the past three years.

A hand suddenly gripped her shoulder from behind, startling her. She turned around to see that Ava and Noah had caught up to them. They could barely see a few feet in any direction, so it was a miracle they hadn't lost each other. Ava clutched Leah's shoulder as they continued walking, with Vincent leading their group through the woods.

It was nearly the end of April, so they hadn't expected a blizzard to interrupt their cross-country camping trip. They had driven all the way to Asheville, North Carolina from Michigan in Vincent's van. The four of them had planned on staying several more days before heading back to the Midwest, but the sudden onslaught of snow had drastically altered their plans.

Earlier in the day, Leah had woken up to Vincent's forced cheery mood, suggesting they spend the day hiking. She had been worried by his sudden change in demeanor from the sullen wreck he had been for weeks now, so she hastily accepted his idea.

Somehow, Leah had convinced Ava and Noah to join them; although she had basically dragged them out of the warmth and comfort of their sleeping bags into the chilly morning air. Leah still wasn't sure why Ava and Noah had agreed to the trip at all. Neither of them was an outdoorsy person—not that Leah was, either.

Leah had gone on the trip for Vincent's sake because she knew he needed it. She recognized how thin the thread was that he was hanging on by. The trip would help take his mind off of his dad's suicide. She planned to do whatever she could to make sure he survived this grief. He didn't have to grapple with it alone.

At first, they had hiked in a somber silence while Vincent followed a trail on a map he had packed in his bag. The rest of the group straggled along behind him, as was usually the case. That was one of the many things Leah loved about Vincent—his natural ability to lead others and the fact that most people willingly followed his lead.

Thirty minutes of climbing steep slopes, dodging branches, and avoiding stray obstacles had led to a beautiful panoramic view. Leah gazed out over the mountainside in contentment.

Ava plopped down on a large rock off to the side of the trail. She leaned down and put her dyed platinum-blonde head in her hands. Leah noticed and got Vincent and Noah's attention so they could stop too.

"What's wrong?" Leah asked with concern.

Leah had always been the more responsible twin, entrusted by her parents to watch over her sister. It was second nature to worry about Ava.

Ava huffed and sat up, then crossed her arms over her chest. She sat in tense silence for a moment before answering, "I don't want to go on this frickin' hike anymore."

Noah laughed in a carefree manner and sat down next to Ava. "Babe, take a chill pill. We're almost at the top." He peered at Vincent with a meaningful expression. "Right?"

Vincent glanced down at his map, frowning as he pointed to the trail and traced it with his finger to the end. "No, we still have like two more miles—"

"Vince, come on, man. I just wanted you to tell her that we were almost there. I'm as sick of hearing her complain on this trip as you are," Noah replied in an agitated tone.

Ava leaned over and shoved Noah off the rock. The action must have surprised him because, despite her petite size and Noah's athletic body, Ava made Noah fall to the ground.

Ava stared at Noah sprawled across the grass and burst out laughing, holding her stomach as her laughter rose in intensity. Leah joined her. The sight of her sister's ridiculously in-shape boyfriend laying on the grass because his tiny girlfriend shoved him was too hilarious to ignore.

"Ugh," Noah grunted as he pulled himself to a standing position again. "Guys, it's not that funny," he protested, brushing the grass and dirt from his pants.

Vincent rolled his eyes. "Is everyone done messing around? The plan was to reach the top of the mountain before the afternoon, so we can have a picnic and have time to climb back down. We have to return to the campsite before it's too dark. It's not safe to hike at night out here."

Leah placed a comforting hand on his shoulder and squeezed. "We can keep going, don't worry. Just let us rest for a minute." She pulled her backpack off her shoulders and unzipped the largest compartment. After digging around inside, she pulled out a water bottle, which she handed to Ava. "Here, drink some water. I don't want you to get dehydrated."

Ava accepted the water with a heartfelt "thanks," and chugged half of it before handing it back.

Leah drank some water too, then put the water bottle in her backpack. "Ready?" She glanced at Ava and Noah.

Noah frowned, but Ava nodded, so Leah hoisted her bag back onto her shoulders, and they all continued their hike. By the time they reached the summit, Leah's calves were burning, and she was grateful for a longer break.

They each opened their bags and compiled an assortment of food for a makeshift picnic lunch. After they finished eating, Leah sat on a rock next to Vincent, staring across the mountain to the other side of the woods. Mountain peaks rose steadily in the distance, barely visible through the gloomy fog that had settled in around them. While they ate, the temperature had dropped steadily. Leah shivered in her fleece jacket that wasn't fit for cold weather. A few snowflakes whirled lazily through the air.

"Vince?" She tapped her boyfriend on the shoulder.

"Hmm?" He gazed down at her. "What's wrong?" he said when he noticed her expression.

Leah pointed to the melting snowflakes on her jacket and looked up at him. His expression soon mirrored hers.

"Pack up everything," Vincent ordered the others as he threw the last of his food and belongings into his bag.

Everyone followed suit.

"Why is it so cold? I didn't think it could snow here in the spring." Ava crinkled her button nose. She was wearing mittens, with a beanie pulled over her wavy, blonde hair.

Noah shrugged. "Just like Michigan, I guess. Bogus weather."

"Snow wasn't on the weather forecast before we left, though," Leah interjected.

Vincent stood, hefted his pack onto his back, and tightened the straps. "We need to get back to the campsite before the snow gets worse."

Ava's eyes widened, and she stopped repacking her bag. "*Worse*? Like, you think there's going to be a blizzard or something?"

"I'm not sure. Like Leah said, a snowstorm wasn't in the weather forecast before we left for this trip, but it's not like we've had access to the news since we've been in the mountains," Vincent replied.

"What if we can't make it back in time?" Leah strode along beside Vincent as they started the descent back to the campsite.

Vincent's expression turned grim. "Then we'll have to make a shelter until the snowstorm passes. But that's the worst-case scenario, so don't worry."

Despite their quickened pace, the snow continued to fall, and the sky darkened as the storm rolled in. Leah wiped off her glasses and realized she could barely make out more than a few feet in front of her. The snow swirled around them and came down in thicker chunks, sticking to Leah's long hair. She followed Vincent blindly, wondering if the others were having as much trouble seeing as she was.

They kept moving down the trail, with Vincent intermittently swearing as he struggled to read the map.

Leah wrapped her arm around Vincent and tried to read the map over his shoulder. He had pulled his flashlight from his bag and was shining it on the map, scanning the area where he thought they were.

"Shit," Vincent muttered.

"What?" Leah asked.

Vincent moved the flashlight away from the map and back to the trail. "I'm not sure where we are."

Noah chuckled. "Great, so you got us lost?"

Ava came up to Leah, fiddling with her mittens. "What are we going to do?"

Leah dropped her arm from Vincent and hugged Ava. "It will be okay. We'll figure something out."

"No, we won't." Noah pointed at Vincent. "This idiot got us lost. Let me see the map. I'll figure it out."

"Fine! If you think you can do better, be my guest." Vincent handed the map and flashlight to Noah. He stood with his arms folded across his chest.

After a few minutes of more bickering, Noah gave the map and flashlight back to Vincent. "Okay, okay. We're lost. I can't tell where we are, either. I think we should follow the trail until we reach a cabin or a campsite."

"Yeah, we couldn't have wandered too far from the original path. We'll look for a landmark or a sign to help us. We might run into other campers or hikers on the way," Vincent said.

They wandered down the mountain, hoping they wouldn't be stranded out in the open. All they cared about was finding a safe place to seek shelter until the snow stopped.

Leah shuddered and tried not to think about what would happen if they couldn't find somewhere safe to stay for the night. What if they froze to death?

The air had become increasingly colder, and they had nothing with them that could keep them warm enough until the morning. They each wore regular hiking clothes, leggings and long-sleeve shirts, light fleece jackets over their shirts, and hiking boots. Their tent, sleeping bags, and warmer layers of clothes were back at the campsite.

Finally, she couldn't keep her thoughts to herself any longer and spoke up, "What if we can't find shelter?"

Vincent abruptly stopped and Leah bumped into his back, bracing herself with a hand against him.

"Stop for a minute!" Vincent yelled, fighting to be heard over the ever-increasing wind. He turned around to face the group. "Don't worry, we'll be fine. There have to be cabins or other people out here. I'm sure we weren't the only ones camping this week."

Ava and Noah stepped closer to them, and they all huddled together to hear each other over the howling wind.

"But we weren't staying at an official campsite, so no one will know if we get lost!" Ava cried, her chestnut-brown eyes crinkling.

Noah patted Ava on the shoulder. "We aren't lost, just a little off the trail. We'll be fine."

"How will we be fine if we have to sleep out in the open in a snowstorm?" Ava asked, her voice rising in pitch and sounding hysterical.

"Hey, we won't have to sleep out here. We'll figure something out. Vincent will make sure we're safe," Leah said, grabbing her sister's mittened hand to hold in comfort. She needed to fight back her own fear for her sister's sake.

"Come on, we should get going if we want to find a place to sleep for the night," Vincent commanded.

His unusually cold demeanor startled Leah, but she assumed the situation was stressing him out. They would all feel better if they found a warm shelter, she reasoned.

The four teenagers continued their hike, hoping for a miracle. Leah's fingers felt numb through her gloves, and her thin coat was barely protecting her from the wind and snow. She trudged on, dreaming of a mug of hot chocolate and a warm blanket.

After they had carefully traipsed down the mountainside for a while, Vincent called out to them. "Look! Do you see that? A cabin!"

Leah's gaze drifted to the spot where Vincent pointed. She was nearsighted, so she struggled to see what Vincent had spotted. "Where?"

Vincent pointed again, and as they ventured closer, Leah saw a moderately sized log cabin several hundred feet off the trail. Smoke rose from the chimney, signifying a fire going, and more importantly, that there was most likely someone inside.

"We'll knock on the door and ask if we can come inside until the storm passes. I'm sure they'll understand," Vincent said.

Leah and Ava exchanged concerned glances.

"We're just going to knock on a stranger's door and ask if we can stay with them? Are you for real?" Leah slowed her pace as she considered the idea. She rubbed her arms to warm herself.

"Don't worry, we'll protect you." Noah grinned, gesturing to himself and Vincent. Noah stepped up to the door of the cabin and knocked.

Leah waited for someone to answer, hoping someone would let them inside, fearing their fate if they did, and what would happen if they didn't. The snow whirled around them, the storm intensifying as they waited.

Chapter 2: Camille

Camille sat on the well-worn couch, legs folded underneath her, reading a worn paperback with the fire blazing from the stone fireplace in front of her. Her small terrier mix, Brody, lay on the couch next to her, dozing. She reread the same sentence, and her eyes involuntarily shut as weariness overcame her.

Several alarming things happened all at once, further adding to the chaos when she awoke. The paperback book slipped from her hands and landed with a thud on the scuffed floorboards. A series of knocks sounded on the front door. Brody began barking aggressively. Camille startled out of her restless sleep, assuming the knocks had been part of her dream.

Camille picked up the book and placed it on the coffee table, then she stood from the couch and raised her arms above her head, stretching them to their full length. She went into the small kitchen to brew a pot of tea when another knock came from the front door. Pausing as she heated the tea kettle, she stared at the door, tilting her head. Brody jumped up from the couch and followed her to the door.

"Well, who on earth could that be, Brody?" she mumbled. She smoothed down her frizzy hair.

Brody growled as Camille unlatched the deadbolt, then unlocked the second lock. She turned the doorknob and opened the door. Her eyes widened in surprise.

Four young people—teenagers, by the looks of them—stood on her doorstep as snow fell heavily around them. A thick blanket of snow had already covered the grass and garden, and she could barely see to the trail that she knew wasn't more than several hundred feet away.

"Hello?" Camille kept her hand on the doorknob, ready to slam the door shut if necessary.

"Hi," the shorter of the two men said, stepping forward and extending his hand to shake as Brody barked at him. "I'm Vincent. This is my girlfriend, Leah, her twin sister Ava, and Ava's boyfriend, Noah. Nice to meet you."

"Nice to meet you too," Camille replied warily, waving off her dog. "Don't worry, he's harmless. Just overprotective of me. How can I help you?"

What did these people want from her? No one was supposed to know she was here. It was what she had wanted. No interruptions, no people, nothing to distract her from writing her novel.

Vincent cleared his throat and glanced around at his girlfriend and friends. "Um, sorry to disturb you like this... We hate to impose, but we really don't—"

The wind howled, and Camille could barely make out what he was saying. "Come in, come inside then." She hastily ushered them into her cabin before the snow and cold could invade her warm sanctuary.

They followed her inside, and Camille shut the door behind them. She stood in the living room, which was the first room upon entering the cabin, and turned to face them. "Now, what were you saying?"

"Sorry about this," Vincent began. "We were hiking when the snowstorm started. We tried to find our way back to our campsite, but we must have gotten turned around along the way. The snow is coming down pretty hard now. Would it be all right if we stayed here for a few hours? Just until the storm passes?"

Leah clung to Vincent's arm, her eyes darting around the cabin.

Camille pursed her lips and stared inquisitively at the group of people who had interrupted her peaceful alone time. "I'm not sure."

"Please," Leah begged her. "We promise it will only be until the snowstorm is over. This is the first place we came across. I don't know how we would find our way back to the campsite with the visibility so bad. It's impossible to see more than a few feet in any direction."

Camille pondered the situation. She didn't like the thought of letting four strangers into her home, especially while her husband was away. But surely, the storm would end soon, and they would leave.

"All right then," she replied at last. "You can stay. But only until the storm passes."

Chapter 3: Leah

Leah peered around the main room of the small cabin, anxiously inspecting their refuge for the next few hours. *Or longer*, Leah thought, wondering how long the snowstorm would last. Although she didn't relish the idea of staying in a stranger's cabin, they needed to be prepared to hunker down for the night. She knew little about Asheville's weather and wasn't sure how intense the storm would be.

In the center of the room, a blazing fireplace took up nearly the entire wall. Off to the side, a red couch and a plaid armchair were the only seating options. A coffee table was positioned in front of the couch. The floorboards were wooden and well-worn with age. A frayed beige rug with bold geometric shapes sprawled across most of the room, covering the floor. Leah wandered over to the far wall and spotted several framed pictures. In one picture, a younger Camille grinned up at a tall man with long, dark hair who had his arms wrapped around her.

Leah gazed at the picture with the man in it for longer than the others. She glanced at Vincent, then back to the picture, and shook her head as if to rid herself of the strange thought. She must be imagining things.

Underneath the framed photos, an antique writing desk stood proudly with a typewriter on top of it as the main area of interest. The typewriter looked brand new, but Leah didn't see a familiar brand name on it. She wasn't close enough to read the inscription on the front, but an engraving glistened on the typewriter. Leah inched closer and squinted at the words: *"Videte omnes qui tenent potestatem clavium, quia potestatem habebunt creandi et destruendi."*

Was that Latin? What did it mean?

Various papers, pens, and files were also scattered across the desk. A plush purple chair was pushed against the desk. Mismatched and eclectic, but cozy, seemed to be the theme of the cabin.

"Well, have a seat." Camille gestured to the faded red couch.

They all squeezed onto the couch, which barely had enough room for the four of them. Leah partially sat on Vincent's lap, and Ava sprawled across Noah.

Camille sat in the oversized plaid armchair. Her terrier immediately jumped onto her lap, curling himself up as small as possible and continuing to growl at them in a low tone. "Shh, Brody, you're fine." Camille stroked his small head, and his growling eventually subsided.

"How old is he?" Leah smiled and gestured at the dog.

"Oh, let's see. I adopted him in '81... So, he's seven now." Camille petted her dog fondly. "Why were you out in the woods during a snowstorm?"

Noah spoke up, patting Vincent on the back. "Because of this asshole."

Camille gasped audibly, and her hand flew to her mouth. She stood from the armchair, and Brody fell off her lap with a surprised yelp. "No, no, this won't do." She shook her head rapidly back and forth, pacing the room. "No, this won't do at all."

"Uh, sorry, but what's wrong?" Ava asked timidly, trying to become more comfortable in her squished position between Leah and Noah on the couch.

"The *swearing!*" Camille yelled, pointing an accusatory finger at

Noah.

Leah glared at Noah, wanting him to apologize to Camille so they could stay in her cabin.

"Oh, sorry about that," Noah replied sheepishly, scratching the back of his head. His cheeks had turned bright red.

"If you're going to stay here, then there are a few rules you'll have to abide by." Camille continued pacing, and Brody followed her, seeming almost as agitated as Camille as he struggled to keep up with her. "First, I don't tolerate swearing in my home. Not at all. No exceptions. Second, if you stay here, then I expect help with chores and cleaning up. I don't like messes. I keep a clean house. Third, and probably the most important rule, don't ever, under any circumstances, touch my typewriter or read any of my papers on my desk."

Vincent nodded. "That seems fair."

Noah and Ava both shrugged uncaringly.

"Absolutely," Leah replied. "We'll follow your rules. Thank you for your hospitality, Camille. We really appreciate it. I don't know what we would have done if we hadn't stumbled across your cabin."

Camille finally stopped pacing and settled down in her armchair again. This time, Brody stretched out on the rug in front of the fireplace. He seemed to want to avoid his owner's lap after she had startled him earlier.

Camille smiled at the four of them. "Of course. As long as you follow my rules, we'll get along fine."

***

"So, that's how we ended up here at your cabin," Vincent finished explaining what had happened.

Camille nodded. "That's quite a long journey from Michigan. You all must be exhausted. When's the last time you ate?"

"We ate a picnic lunch on the top of the mountain earlier today, but that was like forever ago. I'm starving," Ava whined, holding her hands across her stomach.

"*Ava!*" Leah chastised her sister.

"What? If this is her home, then she probably has a stash of food," Ava replied, twirling her blonde hair around her finger.

"I do. I have dried goods in the kitchen and a fridge and freezer full of food," Camille said. "In any case, I'm happy to bring out some food for you. I have plenty. Enough to last me three more months."

Camille stood and headed into a room to the right of the sitting area, presumably the kitchen.

When Camille was out of the room, Leah turned to her sister, which was quite a feat considering how tangled together they all were on the couch. "You can't just show up at someone's house and demand food, Ava!"

Ava untwisted her hair from her finger and rolled her eyes. "Yeah, whatevs. I know you're all hungry too. Someone had to say something."

"We still have some snacks from earlier in our bags," Vincent reminded them, gesturing to the bags.

"Well, duh, but we should save that food in case it takes a while to find the campsite when we leave," Noah suggested, attempting to shift Ava over so he could stretch out his legs.

"True. We don't know where we are or how far away the campsite is. We could be miles away. Maybe Camille knows the area and can help us out. Vince, you still have the map, right?" Leah said.

Vincent grabbed his backpack, unzipped it, and began digging around inside the large compartment. He wrestled out a folded map. "Yup, got it."

"Okay, good. So, we can ask Camille for help, figure out which direction to head, and be back at the campsite tonight," Leah said with a satisfied smile.

Things would work out. They had to. This trip was supposed to fix things, not make them worse.

"Works for me," Noah said.

"Wait. I'm not sure about that. It's already dark outside, and it will be much more difficult to see. It was already hard enough with the snow. I think we should ask Camille if we can crash here for the night, then we'll leave in the morning," Vincent suggested, taking charge in the way he always did.

Ava groaned. "I don't want to stay in some random cabin! How do we know she isn't like a serial killer or—"

Camille reentered the room, carrying a serving platter full of food. She set it down on the coffee table in front of them and proudly stepped back to let them help themselves to the food. Camille had piled the tray with an assortment of meats, cheeses, crackers, grapes, olives, and several small bowls of dip. "I hope this will suffice."

"Looks perf!" Ava cheerily examined the food.

"Thank you, Camille. This is very kind of you," Leah said, moving toward the food as well.

Vincent agreed, "Thanks, Camille."

Noah had already helped himself and was munching happily on a piece of prosciutto. When Ava nudged him, he thanked Camille with a mouth full of food. Camille stared at him with a mixture of unease and disgust on her face, then returned to her plaid armchair.

After they had eaten enough, Vincent trudged over to the window and peeked outside, then came back to the couch and cleared his throat. Camille turned her attention to him expectantly.

"It hasn't stopped snowing yet, and it's dark outside. Would it be all right if we stayed here for the night? We'll leave first thing in the morning, and we'll help clean up the food and anything else you need in return," Vincent said.

"Vince and I can gather more wood for the fire before we leave too,"

Noah offered.

"That would be lovely," Camille replied. "As far as staying the night..." She frowned, sitting up straight in the armchair and gazing into the fire as if searching for an answer to the predicament. "I'm not sure that's a good idea."

Leah chimed in, "I promise we won't be a bother. We can sleep out here, and we'll be quiet. We won't mess up your routine, and we'll leave as soon as the sun rises."

Camille continued to gaze into the fire, stroking her chin as if in deep thought. "I suppose. If it's just for the one night. But that's it. You'll be on your way as soon as it's safe to travel?"

"For sure, we'll leave the second we're able to. I just want to go home and veg out for a week. This entire trip has been awful," Ava complained.

"Then why did you beg me to come with you?" Noah asked, eyebrows raised in disbelief.

"Because... well, it's Vincent..." Ava stuttered.

Leah shushed her. "It's not important. We'll end the trip early and head home tomorrow. It's impossible to camp with this much snow, anyway. The tent and sleeping bags can't withstand temperatures this low."

"I guess we should have realized it can snow in the mountains in the spring still, just like in Michigan." Vincent frowned as he stared at the rapidly falling snow outside. "When we checked the weather forecast before we left last week, it only predicted sunshine and a chance of rain. Nothing like this. We weren't prepared for a snowstorm."

Camille smiled and responded cryptically, "Sometimes storms come out of nowhere. Almost as if they're conjured with magic."

Chapter 4: Camille

Three hours later, Camille yawned and stretched, glancing over at Brody, who was still laying in front of the dying fire. The embers faintly glowed, barely emitting any heat. "Time for bed, I think."

The blonde girl—Ava—had dozed off and her head rested on her boyfriend's shoulder. He gently shook her, waking her up.

"My room is the master bedroom, the bigger of the two, but there's a spare bedroom too. You're welcome to sleep in there or on the couch out here. I'll let you decide who wants to sleep where, but I'm off to bed. Goodnight, all."

"Wait—you're staying here all by yourself? I thought maybe there was someone else here with you in one of the other rooms," Ava said sleepily as she rubbed her eyes.

"I'm working on my next novel. I need peace and quiet to concentrate and finish it," Camille said, standing and heading toward Brody, who stretched out in front of the formerly blazing fire. He peeked his head up when he heard her approach.

"Don't you get lonely?" Leah asked.

"No, not really. Besides, I'm not alone. I have Brody. He's much better company than most people are." Camille laughed and patted Brody on the head affectionately.

Camille exited the room and headed to her bedroom, with Brody trotting after her. She shut the bedroom door and made her way over to the ridiculous king-size bed that was much too large for one person. She remembered picking it out with Robert years ago. He had insisted on buying the enormous bed, but now that she was alone, it was even more ridiculous. Too much room reminding her that he wouldn't sleep with her ever again.

Camille sighed and picked up her neatly folded pajamas from the bed. Out in the sitting room, her guests whispered in agitated tones. She assumed they were fighting over which couple got to sleep in the spare bedroom. She smiled to herself. This was already turning out better than she had expected. Telling them to choose for themselves where they slept had been a clever spur-of-the-moment decision.

"We're going to have fun, aren't we, Brody?" Camille said in a high-pitched voice, eliciting excited tail wags from the little terrier who had no clue what she was saying. He jumped onto her bed and curled up by her feet, staring up at her expectantly. She bent down close to him to scratch behind his ears. "Yes, lots of fun with our new guests."

***

The next morning, Camille awoke before the sun had even graced the sky with its presence. She turned the doorknob of her bedroom slowly and tiptoed out into the main room. Vincent was on the couch with Leah lying on his chest. Ava and Noah must have won the fight for the bedroom then.

Camille grinned and walked over to her typewriter, leaning across the desk and lightly stroking the keys with fondness. She studied the Latin inscription on the typewriter: *"Videte omnes qui tenent potestatem clavium, quia potestatem habebunt creandi et destruendi."* When she found the typewriter, she questioned the inscription to the elderly man who gave it to her. She could never repay him for what he had done for her. She had learned so much since the typewriter first came into her possession.

"Hello, old friend," she whispered, caressing the keys once more. "Later," she assured the typewriter, as if making a promise to a lover.

Camille passed Leah and Vincent on the couch to head to the kitchen. Brody joined her. He sprawled out on the rug in front of the sink and lazily watched her prepare breakfast, with his eyes opening every so often to make sure she was still there.

As she bustled around in the kitchen, brewing coffee and frying eggs, she knew her guests wouldn't be able to sleep much longer. The scent of freshly brewed coffee and oil from the cooking eggs hung heavy in the air.

The teenagers had promised they would leave before the sun rose, but as Camille slid the eggs onto a plate, she darted a glance out the window to see that the sun had already fully risen in the sky.

In the kitchen, there was only a small, circular wooden table against the wall underneath the window with two matching wooden chairs. Each chair had a cushion on it for padding; otherwise, the wooden chairs were quite uncomfortable. She set her breakfast and coffee mug on the table and sat in a chair. Brody lay by her feet, hoping for Camille to drop scraps for him.

She shooed him away. "Go eat your breakfast, Brody. You can't have people food," she scolded him.

Camille sipped her coffee and stared out the window, watching the sun shine as the pink and orange hues overtook the sky. The snowstorm was over.

"Morning, Camille." Vincent entered the kitchen, running his fingers through his dark hair, which was gathered into a ponytail. "Oh, I thought I heard you talking to someone."

"No, just me in here. And Brody, of course."

"Right. I'll wake the others, and we'll be gone soon."

Camille took another sip of her coffee and smiled. "There's no rush. Why don't you join me for breakfast first?" She gestured to the chair across from her, where there was another plate of eggs and a second mug full of coffee. "I hope you're a coffee drinker."

Vincent nodded in acknowledgement. "How'd you guess I would be the first one up?" he asked as he cut into a fried egg.

"You remind me so much of my husband," Camille whispered. "Robert was an early riser. He had the same long, dark hair as you. He also insisted on wearing it in a ponytail." She shook her head and laughed warmly.

Vincent darted a sympathetic glance at her. "*Was*? Is he—?"

"Oh, no, no, no. I didn't mean for you to get the wrong idea. He's away on a business trip at the moment. This time, it's Japan. He travels quite a bit for work. I miss him so much while he's away, though."

"I can imagine." Vincent took a bite of the egg.

"What about you? You have family back in Michigan, I assume?" Camille changed the subject.

"Oh, uh... Actually, my dad died recently. That's why we took this trip." Vincent put his fork down and stared sullenly at his half-eaten egg.

Camille leaned over the table to pat Vincent's hand. "I'm so sorry to hear that. Grief is never easy."

"Yeah, especially when it's unexpected. What do you do for fun out here all by yourself? It must be lonely."

"I have Brody to keep me company, and my writing keeps me busy," Camille replied with a sniff.

"What are you writing about?" Vincent asked.

Leah entered the kitchen, rubbing her eyes.

"Morning, Leah," Vincent greeted his girlfriend cheerfully, dropping the conversation with Camille to turn his full attention to Leah.

Leah mumbled an incoherent response that Vincent somehow understood. He asked Camille where the coffee mugs were and filled one for Leah. While Leah stood awkwardly next to the table since there wasn't another chair, Vincent grabbed his girlfriend around the waist. He pulled her onto his lap, then kissed her on top of her head. Leah's grumpy expression instantly vanished, and she giggled, setting her coffee mug carefully on the table so she didn't spill.

Camille had finished her breakfast and coffee and didn't want to witness the gag-worthy show of affection between the young couple, so she took her leave and retreated to her bedroom. She changed out of her pajamas and put on more suitable clothes for the day.

By the time she had brushed her teeth and arranged her hair into a French braid, Ava and Noah were also awake and sitting on the couch. Noah was tugging a small rope toy, and Brody was trying to snatch it from him.

Camille cleared her throat noisily, so everyone stared at her. "I believe the agreement was that you would be out of my home by the time the sun rose. I'm a gracious host, though, so if you would like to stay longer, you're welcome to." She stared out the window and at the sun, which was shining brightly and stubbornly as if to emphasize her point.

Noah and Ava stood from the couch. Brody whined, probably because Noah had stopped playing with him. The small dog wagged his tail impatiently.

"Sorry, we'll get out of your hair. Just let us grab our stuff," Ava apologized and darted off into the spare bedroom, with Noah following quickly behind.

Leah and Vincent joined Camille in the main room. Their packed bags stood waiting beside the front door, and they looked like they were ready to go.

"I apologize for my sister and her boyfriend. Vince and I always wake up early and stick to a schedule, but they're not used to doing that," Leah explained, shaking her head.

"It's fine," Camille said. She pursed her lips and sighed. "I must get some writing done. On a normal day, I would have written several thousand words by now."

"Oh, we don't mind if you write! We'll just wait here for Ava and Noah," Leah said.

Camille glanced at Vincent for his reaction.

"We understand your writing is important. Better get those words down." Vincent grinned.

"Of course." Camille pulled out her chair and settled into the plush comfort, resting her fingers just above the keys of the typewriter.

The circumstances of the past twelve hours—the four strangers showing up at her cabin and the snowstorm that came out of nowhere—inspired her, and the words seemed to tumble out of her faster than she could type them.

"Oh, this will be perfect," she mumbled. "I love a good plot twist."

Chapter 5: Leah

Ava and Noah finally returned from the spare room with their bags in their hands. Ava's face was unusually pale, and she had pulled her normally sleek hair back into a messy ponytail.

"Are you okay?" Leah moved toward her sister and scrutinized her.

"Yeah, just feeling a little sick." Ava held her hand against her stomach and groaned.

Leah wasn't sure if Ava was being her usual dramatic self or if something was seriously wrong. She glanced at Vincent to see his reaction, but he merely shrugged.

Noah chuckled and put his arm around Ava. "She's fine. You know she can be a wimp when she has so much as a headache."

Ava's gaze went to the scuffed wooden floor, but she ignored Noah's comment. "Let's get going. The sooner we get home, the better."

Leah's eyebrows drew together in concern. "Okay."

During their conversation, Camille had still been typing on her typewriter, but she paused and turned around to face them. She pushed back her chair from the desk and stood. She headed toward the door, waiting for them to leave without saying a word.

"Come on, let's refill our water bottles and get on the road." Leah picked up her backpack and hoisted it onto her shoulders.

The others copied her.

"Time to head out. Thanks again for everything, Camille," Vincent said. He reached for the doorknob and turned it slowly.

"It was my pleasure, Vincent. Have a safe journey home," Camille said with her eyes shining.

Vincent pulled the door open to reveal several feet of thickly packed snow, with more snowflakes falling.

The sky darkened ominously as Leah, Ava, and Noah followed Vincent outside.

Chapter 6: Camille

A small smile played across Camille's face as everyone reacted to the snow. Twenty minutes ago, the sun had been shining brightly, and the grass was growing vibrant and green. The sky was clear, but it was becoming a dark mauve color as the snow fell in thick flakes, blanketing the grass. *They can't leave now. They'll have to stay.*

"Oh, my!" Camille's voice oozed with concern as she poked her head outside. "Where did all this snow come from? I thought it had warmed up overnight." She dug her fingernails into the scratched-up door frame, ignoring the claw marks covering it. "Are you sure it's safe for you to venture out there?"

Vincent gritted his teeth, but hesitated before taking another step outside. "We don't have a choice. We have to get home. All our stuff is out there still. We have to find our campsite and pack up everything."

Leah squeezed Vincent's shoulder. "I don't know, Vince. It looks pretty bad out there, and we still don't know how far we are from the campsite. We didn't have time to ask Camille for directions." She glanced at Camille with a half-smile.

"I know this area very well. I would be happy to give you an idea of where my cabin is so you can see where you are and find your way. Do you have a map?" Camille said.

Vincent nodded stoically and shut the front door. The others followed him back inside, shivering after being exposed to the winter wonderland. Vincent pulled off his bag and unzipped it, fumbling around for the map. When he found it, he unfolded it and walked back into the main room, spreading the map out to its full length on the coffee table.

"So, where are we right now?" Vincent asked.

Camille and the others joined him, surrounding the table. Camille huddled close to Vincent under the pretense of showing him her cabin's location. Vincent smelled like a mix of outdoorsy musk and coffee. She inhaled the scent, savoring it to remember later. *Just like she wanted. Just like Robert.*

She stared at the map for a moment, orienting herself, and found the main road near the cabin. "My cabin is here." She pointed helpfully to a spot slightly off the main road. The road her cabin was on didn't have a name because it was a private road. It was a good thing she knew the area well, so she could help them. "Which campground were you staying at?"

Ava shot Vincent a triumphant look. "Oh my God. I told you we should have stayed at an actual campground! Then we could find it. Instead, we're going to be lost forev—"

"Ava, will you stop complaining for two seconds?" Vincent snapped, throwing up his arms.

Leah patted Ava on the arm. Camille did the same to Vincent.

"Calm down, honey. It's okay," Camille said in a soothing tone to Vincent.

Leah narrowed her eyes. Camille made eye contact with Leah and smiled, showing her perfectly straight, white teeth like a wolf to a lamb. Leah had no clue whom she was messing with. Camille would fight for Vincent if she had to.

Noah's gaze bounced back and forth between the two women, most likely chanting *fight, fight, fight* in his head. He seemed like the type who would enjoy watching two half-naked women brawl in a mud pit. Camille didn't think he dared to voice his thoughts during a tense situation, though. Thank the Lord for that.

"We didn't stay at a campground. We were camping in the woods," Vincent said. "I think our tent is around here." He pointed to a place on the map that was three miles west.

"Great. So, you don't even know where our tent is?" Ava groaned and plopped onto the couch. She crossed her arms over her chest.

"Ava, I swear—" Vincent started.

"Everyone, stop!" Leah yelled, surprising the rest of the group. "Obviously, we have to find the campsite and Vincent's van, but we need to decide if that's the best move right now. This second snowstorm came out of nowhere. I don't know if walking three miles in a snowstorm is a smart idea. What if we get lost again? I highly doubt there are a bunch of cabins around here that we can just drop by for shelter. And even if there are other cabins, they might not have residents home, or they might not be as willing to help us as Camille."

Camille stood from her close position to Vincent, regretting that she no longer had an excuse to be near him, but she had to keep up appearances. For now, at least. "Leah's right. There are only a handful of cabins in this area, and most of the owners are only here in the summer. Their cabins are probably empty right now. If it was my decision, I would tell you to stay here until the snow stops. It never lasts more than a day or two. As soon as it warms up, it should be safe to travel again."

"So, we'll be democratic about this. Let's take a vote. Who wants to walk three miles through the cold and snow to find our campsite and potentially get lost again?" Leah asked.

Vincent and Noah halfheartedly raised their hands.

"And who wants to stay in this warm, cozy cabin until the storm passes?" Leah smiled, then raised her hand.

Ava's hand shot up as well.

"A tie?" Ava groaned again and threw her bag onto the floor. It landed with a startlingly loud thump.

"If I get a vote, then I think you should stay," Camille chimed in. "You're welcome to stay another night. In fact, you can stay as long as you need to. There's no need to rush away. We're just getting to know each other." Camille headed over to the front door, re-latching the dead bolt.

Chapter 7: Leah

Leah knew Vincent wasn't happy with her for going against his decision, but it was the smarter move to stay in Camille's cabin until the snow let up. Venturing out into the woods where the visibility was low would just get them lost again.

She still thought it was crazy the snow had fallen out of nowhere. Just when they thought the snowstorm was over, it had started snowing again, even harder than before. It was their luck that during her first real vacation with Vince, the weather had ruined their trip, and now they were stuck in a stranger's cabin until further notice. It seemed like such a waste to be trapped indoors when they were in a beautiful part of the country that they hadn't been able to fully explore yet. She supposed they should make the best of the situation, and she took it upon herself to cheer everyone up.

"Camille, do you have anything in the cabin we could do for fun? Any activities to pass the time?" Leah scrambled for something to take their minds off of being stuck inside.

"Oh, yes!" Camille clapped her hands together. "I have puzzles and board games... Let me go find them." Camille left the main room and headed down the tiny hallway to the master bedroom.

After Camille left the room, Vincent turned to Leah. He grabbed her arm and pulled her close to him, digging his nails into her arm. "Why did you have to put it to a vote and go against me like that?" he whispered harshly, his lips close to her ear and sending tingles of fear down her spine.

She tried to shake his grip off her arm. "Let go of me!" she said in a normal tone, louder than the one Vincent had used.

Ava and Noah could hear her and stared at them with identical expressions of disapproval.

Noah stepped closer to Vincent and intervened, holding out his hands in front of him. "Hey, dude, let go of Leah. There's no need to get worked up. I was with you about going back outside to find the campsite, but maybe Leah and Ava are right. We can chill here for another day and leave tomorrow. It's not the end of the world if we stay one more night."

Vincent forcefully pulled his hand from Leah's arm. She stumbled from the force, grabbing the doorframe to prevent herself from falling. Her glasses slipped from her face, and she quickly caught them so they didn't fall on the floor. Once her glasses were back in place, she rolled up her sleeve, rubbing her arm where her boyfriend's hand had tightly gripped the skin. She winced as she gingerly touched the sore spot on her arm. Even through her thick sweater, his grip had left a mark.

"Fine." Vincent turned away from the others and went down the hallway, presumably to the guest bedroom.

Leah gave Noah a nod of thanks and stood awkwardly by the front door. She rolled her sleeve back down, covering her arm. "Maybe I should go make sure he's okay..." she mumbled.

"What? No!" Ava protested. "He's being a jerk. Give him some time by himself and let him cool off. He's probably mad that you were right. You know how he gets when he doesn't get his way." Ava rolled her eyes.

Noah chuckled. "He's definitely a sore loser."

Noah tucked Ava's hand into his and pulled her over to the couch, where they sat next to each other. After debating what to do for another moment, Leah finally gave in and sat in the armchair Camille had previously occupied. She leaned back in the chair and sighed.

Brody raced into the room, apparently coming from Camille's bedroom, and jumped up onto Leah's lap, cheering her slightly. She patted his head, and his tail wagged swiftly back and forth.

"You okay?" Ava asked her sister, tilting her head in concern.

Leah stared at the large rug with geometric shapes on it in the middle of the room, not making eye contact with her. Instead, she focused her attention on petting Brody while she replied, "Yeah. I hate when he gets like this."

"Vincent loves you. He just... He doesn't always show it in the best way," Ava attempted to comfort her.

Leah snorted. "Right."

They lapsed into silence, each of them lost in their own thoughts, until Camille came back into the room a few minutes later. In her hands, she held a stack of board games.

"I found some games!" She cheerily set them on the coffee table and grinned at all of them. Then, upon doing a second sweep of the room, she asked, "Where did Vincent go?"

Leah answered glumly, "To the spare bedroom, I think."

Camille frowned and took a tentative step toward Leah. "Is everything all right?"

"Fine," Leah replied, not wanting to elaborate further.

Ava leaned forward to browse the stack of games. "Scrabble?" she suggested.

The rest of them agreed on the choice of game, and Camille set it up.

Two rounds of Scrabble later—Camille won both rounds, much to everyone else's dismay—Vincent wandered into the room and squished in between Ava and Noah on the couch. Ava glared at Vincent and moved around Vincent to be closer to Noah.

"What's your problem?" Vincent huffed and crossed his arms over his chest.

"*My* problem?" Ava scoffed as she stared him down. "Apologize to my sister, and there won't *be* a problem."

Vincent's expression turned guilty, and he glanced at Leah. "I'm sorry, Leah."

"It's okay," Leah replied softly, not wanting to agitate him again. She stroked Brody's head, who was dozing lazily on her lap. All she wanted was for everything to be okay. This trip was supposed to be *fun*, not whatever this was. Everything was going wrong.

"I mean it. I should have listened to you. Going out into the woods in this snowstorm wouldn't just mean risking my life, it would mean risking all of our lives, and that's not worth it. We're safe here," Vincent said, then paused for a second. He gulped before adding, "You were right. I was a jerk." Vincent stood from the couch and ambled over to Leah, leaning down to hug her. "Forgive me?"

A small smile formed on Leah's face, and she allowed Vincent's arms to wrap around her. She nodded. "I forgive you."

Camille's face turned stony, and she busied herself putting away the components of Scrabble. "Is anyone hungry?" She changed the subject after she cleared the game from the coffee table.

Murmurs of agreement that they could eat sounded from everyone, so Camille left for the kitchen to make lunch.

Vincent moved Brody to the ground, then sat in front of Leah and laid his head on her lap. He gazed up at her, smiling as she looked back at him. All was well.

***

Camille brought out an assortment of food and spread it across the coffee table with a stack of plates, telling everyone to help themselves. They each thanked her and grabbed a plate, piling them with food.

As Leah carefully checked out the food, Vincent suddenly made a noise akin to extreme shock or fear—some sort of yelp she had never heard from him before. He pried the plate out of her hand and shoved her away from the table, making her fall to the ground. She nearly sobbed at the idea that Vincent was becoming violent with her and was perhaps abusive, but she caught herself as soon as she saw what Vincent was trying to protect her from.

On the coffee table, on the side furthest from where she had picked out food items to eat, there was an assortment of nuts—the one thing Leah was allergic to. Brody barked at Vincent and bent his head to the ground to lick Leah's face, as if making sure she was okay.

Ava gasped. She must have reached the same conclusion as Vincent. She set her plate down on the table. "You didn't eat anything yet, did you, Leah?" Worry creased Ava's features. She swept her blonde hair back from her face as she surveyed the food and then Leah's plate, checking her twin sister for any signs of an allergic reaction.

"What seems to be the matter?" Camille's eyebrows scrunched together as she appraised the food. "I can assure you all there is nothing wrong with the food. Everything is fresh. Nothing is out of date or expired. It's all perfectly fine."

Vincent extended a hand to help Leah to her feet. "Sorry about that. Are you hurt? I panicked when I saw the nuts."

"I'm fine." Leah accepted Vincent's hand and stood again.

Camille glanced at the nuts and then at Vincent. She shook her head. "The nuts? But there isn't anything wrong—"

"Leah's deathly allergic to nuts," Ava cut in. "Like, if she even comes into contact with them, she could have an anaphylactic reaction."

"I carry an EpiPen with me everywhere I go, just in case," Leah explained. "It's in my bag right now, so I most likely would have been fine, even if I accidentally ate a nut."

Camille pursed her lips, then went back into the kitchen. When she returned a minute later, she held a large black garbage bag in her hands. With several swipes of her arms across the coffee table, she shoveled all the food into the garbage bag. She tied it up and slung it over her shoulder with haste.

"Oh!" Leah said. Her eyes widened, and she put out her hands placatingly. "You didn't have to—"

"No worries, dear. I wouldn't want to accidentally kill one of my guests now, would I?"

Chapter 8: Camille

After setting the heavy garbage bag down on the kitchen floor, Camille swiped a hand across her brow. What was she supposed to do now? They still needed to eat. Would everything be ruined because Leah hadn't eaten the nuts?

Camille pondered her next move, tapping her foot anxiously on the floor, lost in thought. Vincent joined her in the kitchen and startled her out of her thoughts.

"Is Leah all right?" Camille shoved aside the garbage bag, so it was out of the way. She couldn't add the wasted food to the compost pile outside while it was still snowing.

Vincent bit his lip and absentmindedly tightened the elastic around his ponytail, reminding her even more of Robert. He had possessed the same anxious habit. She supposed it made sense for habits like that to pop up in him.

"Yeah, she seems okay for now. Her EpiPen is in her bag if we need it. Although I would rather her not have to use it when we're trapped in a cabin and sheltering from a snowstorm with no way to reach a hospital if there's an emergency." Vincent chuckled nervously. "I came in here to see if I could help fix something else to eat. Sorry you had to waste all that food. We should have mentioned Leah's allergy before you went to all that trouble for us. Normally, it's one of the first things we worry about when we're eating somewhere new. I guess the storm distracted us."

Camille beamed at Vincent and fought the nearly overwhelming urge to run her hands through his long, dark hair, eerily similar to Robert's. She shook her head, trying to dispel any thoughts of her husband. It wouldn't do to think about him since he was gone. It would only make it harder to deal with his absence, and she already missed him about as much as she could handle.

"No worries. It was no trouble," she responded sweetly. "Open that cupboard in front of you—the top one." Camille pointed. "There are snacks in there. I have plenty of food here. Although, unfortunately, I'm sure the snow will severely delay my garden for the year. Fresh vegetables and fruit would have been a delightful addition to my food supplies. I'll worry about that later, though."

Vincent complied, opening the cupboard and pulling out crackers, granola bars, and a variety of other nut-free snacks. He examined the boxes, presumably checking the ingredients in each item for any mention of nuts.

"This is perfect. Thank you, Camille." He gathered the snacks in his arms and carried them to his friends in the next room.

Camille stayed in the kitchen, wondering what she should do with the garbage bag until the snowstorm passed. If the food stayed in there too long, it would probably go bad and start to stink. Well, she could worry about that later too.

"Camille? Aren't you joining us?" Vincent's voice beckoned her.

A smile formed on Camille's face, and she headed toward the living room. "Yes, dear. I'll be right there."

***

They spent the rest of the day eating, playing board games, and playing with Brody, who loved the extra attention. Before they knew it, it was nearly evening, and Camille hadn't written a single word in her new novel all day. At this rate, she would be trapped in her cabin for months before she finished her novel. Each day that passed with the four guests in her cabin, she lost an opportunity to write. She hadn't realized how much having guests would alter her routine.

Camille stood from her position in front of the coffee table and announced, "I need to write."

"Of course. We're sorry for interfering with your schedule," Leah immediately apologized, her gaze falling to the ground as she hung her head.

"If it helps, we can go hang out in the spare bedroom, so you have the room to yourself out here," Vincent suggested. "We'll keep it down so you can concentrate."

Camille nodded her approval, and the foursome retreated into the guest room. Camille dragged Brody's dog bed across the room and placed it underneath the desk. It was Brody's favorite place to nap while she was writing. He curled up in his bed and stared up at her, blinking his big, brown eyes as he fought off sleep.

Camille took a seat and cracked her knuckles, her fingers looming over the keys of the typewriter as she pondered what to write. What trouble should she cook up next?

Several hours later, she glanced at the small clock she kept on her desk, shocked by how much time had passed. She turned her head from side to side, working out the soreness in her neck, and adjusted her position in her chair. While writing, it was so easy to forget that posture was important. How could an author bother thinking about the posture or position of their body while they were creating worlds and inflicting pain and suffering on their characters?

Camille stood from the chair, stretching her arms out to her sides, then bending down to touch her toes. She grabbed her left leg and bent it at the knee, bending it back and grabbing her foot with her hand. She did the same to her right leg and repeated the exercise several times. Her stiffness eased a bit, and she headed toward the fireplace, gazing into the dying embers. She needed to add a few more logs to keep the fire going. Despite the heat running, the cabin was still chilly.

It surprised her that the power hadn't gone out yet, especially because of the snowstorm. Camille remembered how, years ago, Robert had a terrible time when he had asked the power company to wire electricity to their cabin in the middle of the woods. She wondered if the other cabins nearby had power. It was 1988, after all, so surely most of them had power. No one could live without it these days. They all needed their boom boxes, CDs, record players, Nintendo video games, and VCRs.

Camille added more logs to the fire and picked up the fire poker to stoke the fire, then positioned the logs in an ideal position to keep the fire going. As she stepped back to admire the newly blazing fire, Ava tentatively peeked her head around the corner from the hallway.

"Hello, Ava."

"Hi. Uh, I was wondering... I didn't eat much earlier. Were you thinking about cooking dinner?" Ava twirled her blonde hair around her finger and peered at Camille hopefully.

Camille smiled. *This was perfect.* "Of course. Tell the others to come out here."

"Sure."

Camille entered the kitchen and pulled out various cooking utensils, a casserole dish, and ingredients for a recipe. Brody jumped up from his bed and sat at his owner's feet, hoping for Camille to throw him some scraps. She usually did.

She set about making a chicken, vegetable, and rice casserole—simple but filling, and enough food to feed all five of them. After she had browned the chicken and cooked the rice on the stove, she placed the casserole in the oven and set a timer. Then she threw a few cut-up pieces of the cooked chicken into Brody's food dish, which he instantly gobbled up.

Dusting her hands off on a dish towel, she opened the pantry, spotting her wine rack. For several minutes, she debated which wine to choose for the meal and finally decided it didn't matter that much what she picked. She was entertaining a group of teenagers, after all. What did they know about wine? They probably hadn't drunk any decent wines and wouldn't know a merlot from a chardonnay. With a chuckle, she shook her head, then found the corkscrew and pulled out the cork.

By the time she emerged from the kitchen, the others had gathered in the main room of the cabin, lounging on her furniture and enjoying the warmth from the glowing fire. The scent of the casserole baking in the oven wafted throughout the tiny cabin. Everyone laughed as Brody sniffed the air and licked his lips in anticipation.

"Silly dog." Camille patted his head. "No more human food for you today, buddy."

"What's for dinner?" Noah asked, as his stomach grumbled loudly.

Ava laughed and playfully hit Noah's stomach.

"A casserole with chicken, vegetables, and rice in it." Camille shot a glance at Leah. "Don't worry. No nuts this time. It's perfectly safe for everyone to eat."

Chapter 9: Leah

Leah giggled nervously at Camille's comment, thinking about how she had nearly died earlier that day because of her severe nut allergy. Besides, although Camille had thrown away a lot of food earlier, Leah didn't know for sure that those were the only nuts in the cabin. There could be more in the kitchen. If Camille had planned to stay for a few more months, she most likely kept a large supply of dried goods. Nuts could still be listed as an ingredient in other foods.

The paranoia grew in her mind, ramping up her anxiety. But it wasn't like Camille brought out the nuts *on purpose*. They just met her. There was no way Camille could have known about her allergy. She wasn't trying to poison her. It had been an unfortunate incident, but not one borne of malice.

Twenty minutes later, Camille served them each a plate of the chicken casserole.

"Dinner smells delicious," Leah said.

"It looks amazing!" Noah picked up a fork and dug in right away.

They all murmured their thanks, and Camille graciously accepted it. Leah took a hesitant bite of the casserole, glancing at Vincent as she did so. He nodded at her and mouthed the words 'no nuts' with a smile.

Things had been weird between them since Vincent had roughly grabbed her arm, argued with her, and stalked out of the room in anger. He had apologized multiple times, and Leah had forgiven him each time, but she couldn't shake the feeling that something was off. They had been together for two years—long enough to truly know each other. They had found out many annoying habits about each other over time, but none of it had been terrible.

From nearly the beginning, Leah had thought Vincent was perfect for her. He had never raised his voice at her—even when they disagreed—and he had never grabbed her like that before. She told herself it was because of the stressful situation and that he was coming to terms with the fact that all of his family was gone now. That had to be hard to deal with. At least she had Ava and her parents. Vincent had no one except her.

Leah noticed the others had stopped eating. Ava picked at the rest of her food, and Noah offered to finish it for her with a grin. Ava responded with an exaggerated eye roll, but she handed him her half-full plate.

Leah ate a few more bites of the casserole and, after realizing it was simple but delicious, she polished off the rest of the serving Camille had dished up for her.

"Is everyone done? I can take the dishes into the kitchen," Camille said, picking up her plate.

Vincent stood with his empty plate in his hand. "No, Camille, you've done too much for us. Let me do the dishes."

"I appreciate it, Vincent, but you don't know where anything goes."

"Fine, then at least let me help you," Vincent insisted.

Camille agreed and gathered up the dishes. She walked behind Vincent and placed her hand on his back to guide him toward the kitchen. Leah watched them leave the room and sidled up next to Ava on the couch.

Ava rested her head on Leah's shoulder and stifled a yawn. "I'm tired."

"Me too. The past few days have been stressful," Leah responded, yawning as well.

"For real," Noah said. "But we're leaving tomorrow, and we'll be back home before you know it!"

"I can't wait to sleep in my bed again," Ava said with a groan.

"Me. Too," Noah said, emphasizing each word separately. He settled back into the couch with his arms behind his head.

Leah checked to make sure Camille wasn't heading back to them yet and leaned in close to Ava and Noah to whisper, "Does anything seem off to you about Camille?"

Noah shrugged. "Nah, she's just lonely and kinda... what's the word?"

"Eccentric?" Ava suggested.

"Yeah, something like that." Noah shrugged his burly shoulders.

"So, you don't think she's like... hitting on Vincent?" Leah blurted out. Her face heated as she finished her question. She couldn't believe she had said it out loud. It sounded ridiculous.

Noah burst out laughing. "No way!" He drummed his fingers on the arm of the couch as if he was thinking, and said, "I mean, she's kinda hot in a woodsy, book chick type of way, but Vincent wouldn't—"

Ava elbowed Noah in the ribs.

He winced. "Hey!"

"Am I being paranoid?" Leah turned to her sister, ignoring Noah's comment. "It seems like Camille is paying special attention to Vincent and finding excuses to touch him. Did you see how she put her hand on his back when they went into the kitchen together? And when we were perusing the map, she patted Vincent's arm and hovered close to him the whole time."

"Leah, chill out. I think Noah's right," Ava said.

Noah looked surprised that his girlfriend had agreed with him and made a sweeping gesture for her to continue speaking.

"Not just about Camille being kinda hot—because she is—but I know what he meant. It doesn't matter how hot Camille or any other woman is. Vincent loves you. So, even if Camille is flirting with him, that doesn't mean anything. It's not like he's going to cheat on you," Ava said.

Leah nodded, subtly shocked by her sister's sage advice. She gave good dating advice—likely because of how many people she had dated. "You're right. Sorry. Just being paranoid."

Camille and Vincent returned to the main room, with Camille's arm looped through Vincent's. Ava shot a pointed look at Noah.

For about ten seconds, Leah contemplated saying something before deciding it wasn't worth it. All they did was wash dishes and clean up the kitchen. It wasn't like anything had happened between them. Vincent loved her, and besides that, Camille was married and spoke adoringly about her husband. Happily married people didn't cheat on their spouses.

"What's going on in here?" Vincent, oblivious, extracted himself from Camille's hold on his arm and sat beside Leah. He put his arm around her shoulders and pulled her close to him.

"Oh nothing. Just chatting," Leah replied amicably, noting the way Camille glared at her as Vincent nestled close to her.

Leah yawned again, snuggling into Vincent and feeling unreasonably tired. The trip had been stressful, so it shouldn't have been a surprise, but she could barely keep her eyes open. Leah strained her eyes, fighting not to close them. She wondered if everyone else was this exhausted as she stared into the fireplace, feeling strangely enthralled with the fire.

The fire still burned fiercely, even though no one had added new logs in hours. *Strange*, she thought, wondering how long a few logs could burn like that. *When did we last stoke the fire?*

Soon, she couldn't tear her eyes away from the fire. The longer she stared, the more the flames seemed to change. The fire morphed and grew, stretching wider and wider until it could no longer stay contained. It licked up the sides of the stones and widened even more. Without warning, the fire spilled out of the fireplace and began spreading across the room, tearing a path of unstoppable destruction.

Leah jumped onto the couch and screamed, pointing at the fire. Peering around, she wondered why no one else was freaking out. "Quick! We need to do something about the fire!"

Vincent stood up and clutched her hand, pulling her down from the couch. "Leah, are you all right?" he asked, looking her over.

"Vince, there's a fire! It isn't safe here!"

"What are you talking about? The fire is fine." Vincent examined the fireplace, perhaps trying to figure out what Leah was talking about. His eyebrows drew together. "It's just a regular fire."

The fire continued tearing across the room at an alarming speed. Leah couldn't stop herself from screaming as it came closer. Vincent grabbed her and held her in his arms, trying to soothe her. She fought back, wanting to free herself from his embrace and get out of the cabin before they all burned alive. But he held her tightly in a grip she couldn't escape.

"I can put the fire out if Leah doesn't like fire," Camille suggested, getting up and moving toward the fireplace, ready to dispel the flames with a bucket of water nearby.

"No, she's fine." Vincent pulled back from her slightly. He glanced at her again with a questioning look in his eyes.

Why did no one believe her? Couldn't they see it too?

"What's going on?" Ava asked her. "What do you see, Leah?"

"The... the fire is..." Leah stumbled over her words and sank back down onto the couch when Vincent tugged her hand again.

She diverted her gaze from the fire and closed her eyes for a few seconds, willing her heart rate to decrease. After a few deep breaths, she opened her eyes slowly. When she gazed into the fireplace again, the menacing flames had retreated and returned to a regular-sized fire, safely contained in the fireplace. Nothing dangerous about it.

"I thought the fire was out of control," Leah whispered. "It was spreading across the room, so I was worried we would all go up in flames or be trapped in here."

Vincent touched her face gently and guided the back of her head, so she stared at him directly. "Hey, I know you're scared, but I promise we're fine. We're safe now. You're probably overly tired. You just imagined it."

Leah tried to focus on Vincent's hand on her cheek—her sweet boyfriend by her side, along with her sister and Noah. She nodded. She had only imagined it. Of course, the flames hadn't jumped out of the fireplace or torn across the room. That was impossible.

Vincent was right. The cabin was a safe place.

Chapter 10: Camille

"Do we really have to play Scrabble again? What other games do you have?" Ava whined, casting a scowl at the games.

"Hmm, let me check." Camille retreated into her bedroom, searched through the closet, and found a few other games. She went back into the main room and held them out for Ava to see. "These are the last of the games I keep here." She set them on the coffee table next to the others and let everyone peruse the board games.

"Why do you have so many games if you're here by yourself?" Noah asked as he tossed aside checkers. Noah's careless action scared Brody, who had been sleeping peacefully under the coffee table and was rudely awakened when the game hit his tail.

Camille jumped to her feet and grabbed Brody, holding him close to her chest and cooing at him. "Oh, Brody! It's okay, buddy boy. You're fine."

"Sorry," Noah mumbled, rubbing the back of his neck as it flushed red.

Camille kissed the top of Brody's head and placed him gently back on the floor, where he looked up at her, tail wagging, most likely wanting more pets. "Since it's your last night here, I think I'll bring out something special."

With a smile, Camille disappeared into the kitchen to retrieve the wine bottle she had selected earlier, along with five wine glasses and cups—she didn't have enough matching wine glasses—and popped the cork off the wine bottle. Moving slowly, she carried the wine bottle and assorted glasses back out into the main room, taking extra care not to trip and drop them. She placed them carefully on the coffee table and poured wine for everyone.

"There. Enjoy!" She raised her wine glass in the air and then took the first sip, sighing when the flavors exploded in her mouth. A bold red for her bold move.

Her guests exchanged glances between themselves. Camille tried not to smirk. She knew exactly what she had done.

"Uh, thanks for the wine, Camille, but we don't want any," Noah stuttered, holding Ava's hand and rubbing it affectionately.

Ava smiled at him and shook her head. "It's fine, guys. If you want some wine, go ahead."

No one reached for the wine, but Camille took another long gulp of her drink.

Camille stared blankly at Ava. "Oh, I see. You don't drink?"

Ava sighed and looked away from everyone, instead staring up at the ceiling before replying. "No. It's—well, I had a drinking problem for a while."

Camille resisted the urge to say something rude because Ava seemed too young to have a drinking problem, especially one that was so bad she refrained from drinking entirely. However, Camille knew all too well the troubles of indulging in alcohol too often, as Robert had. Her rash judgment wouldn't do in this situation. She needed to show sympathy, to make them think she cared about their wellbeing.

"Oh my goodness! I'm so sorry!" Camille downed the rest of her wine and made a show of gathering up the wine glasses, cups, and the wine bottle. "It wasn't my intention to tempt you. I didn't know! Let me bring all this back into the kitchen."

"Really, it's fine. I haven't touched alcohol in six months." Ava lifted her chin proudly. "If you guys want to drink, go ahead," she repeated, gesturing to the wine bottle.

Vincent plucked a wine glass out of Camille's arms, then grabbed the wine bottle. "In that case, don't mind if I do," he said, pouring himself a sizeable glass of wine.

Leah glowered at her boyfriend. "Vince!"

"What? Ava said it was fine. She wouldn't lie about that." Vincent turned to Ava as he sniffed the wine, determining the scent. He swirled it around in his glass before taking a sip. "Right?"

Ava nodded. "Seriously, don't let my addiction stop you from enjoying some wine. Go for it."

"But it doesn't seem very smart for you to be in a toxic environment," Leah protested.

Ava stubbornly crossed her arms over her chest. "It's my decision. I won't be tempted or whatever. I don't even like wine. Beer was my drink," she said with a smirk.

"Oh fine, screw it," Leah responded, grabbing a wine glass and holding it out so Vincent could fill it.

Camille smiled gleefully and set everything back on the coffee table.

"Noah?" Vincent waved the half-empty wine bottle around. "You want some?"

Noah peered at Ava, gauging her reaction, then firmly shook his head. "Nah, it's chill." He put his arm around Ava and kissed her loudly on the cheek.

"If you want to drink—" Ava started.

"Nope, I'm good," Noah replied, tousling Ava's long, blonde hair.

Ava protested and tried patting her hair back to normal.

Leah sat on the floor in front of the coffee table, sipping her wine. She perused the games again and slid one game out of the stack. "Trivial Pursuit?"

Noah laughed and pumped his fist in the air. "I'll crush you all!"

Camille joined in his laughter and leaned forward eagerly to set up the game on the table. "Not if I crush you first."

***

After the game ended, Camille spoke up with her idea, "I thought you all could sleep in the spare bedroom and my bedroom tonight. One couple in each bedroom."

The four of them stared at her, but no one spoke. They most likely wondered why she had suggested the idea, so she elaborated.

"I appreciate that you all gave me some time to write earlier, but I really need to write more today. I have a deadline to stick to and—"

"We don't want to take over your bedroom, though! You'll want to sleep at some point tonight. It's not like you can write all night," Vincent insisted. "Leah and I can sleep out here. We'll be quiet, so you can write."

Leah glared at Vincent, and her upper lip protruded into a pout. "I don't know if—"

Camille interrupted her, "It's fine. My writing would disturb you if you slept out here. My typewriter is rather loud. Sleep in my bedroom. I'm perfectly fine with the couch tonight. I take naps on it all the time, so I know it will suffice for one night."

"Are you sure?" Vincent ran his hand through his ponytail.

Camille nodded resolutely. "Of course. This way, I'll be able to write without any interruptions, and you all should be able to get a good night's sleep before leaving in the morning. You'll want to be well-rested for the long journey ahead of you."

"Okay, well, we really appreciate this," Vincent said with a glance at Leah.

"Yeah. Thanks, Camille," Leah added when she noticed Vincent staring at her. "Don't worry. We'll be out of your hair in the morning. This time tomorrow evening, you'll be back to your normal routine, and we'll be long gone."

Camille blinked several times, realizing Leah was right. The snow had melted, the temperature climbing over the course of the day. By the morning, it should be safe for them to travel. They would find their tent and van, then go home, leaving her forever. She would be alone again. Tonight, Camille would have at least a few hours to write, depending on how early the others went to sleep, but it should be enough time.

She needed to make sure they didn't go anywhere tomorrow. Not if she could help it.

Chapter 11: Leah

Leah yawned and covered her mouth with her hand.

"Tired?" Vincent asked as he stroked her hair.

"Mmhmm. Can we go to sleep soon?" Leah pleaded, staring up at him.

Ava was sitting on Noah's lap with her arms curled around his neck, and her eyes kept closing. Noah was snoring loudly. Apparently, everyone was tired. Everyone except Camille, that is.

Camille appeared alert, her eyes sharp and focused on every detail. Leah wondered if that was a writer thing—to scrutinize every situation, each person's words and actions. Maybe she filed it all away for her books. Where else would she get inspiration when she was all alone out here in the woods for months at a time? That sounded like a nightmare to Leah.

"You can sleep in my bed, Vincent," Camille said. "And you too, of course, Leah," she added quickly.

"Thanks," Leah said with a small smile. *What's up with her?*

"I'll show you where everything is," Camille offered, standing and ushering Leah and Vincent down the hallway.

"Oh, that's unnecessary. I'm sure we'll be fi—" Leah said.

"No, *I insist.*" Camille pressed her lips together, marching down the hallway in front of them.

"Thanks, Camille." Vincent beamed at her with his radiant smile.

Leah and Vincent followed Camille into the master bedroom, where she flicked the light switch on, illuminating a small but cozy room decorated similarly to the rest of the cabin. A king-size bed, too big for the room, dominated most of the space. A navy-blue quilt covered the bed with matching pillow shams. Another blanket was folded on top of the quilt. The room smelled like vanilla. Leah bent over to the nightstand and picked up a candle, sniffing it.

There was only one window with heavy room-darkening curtains shrouding the inhabitants from the outside world. A few framed landscape pictures hung on the walls, which were painted a soft lilac. The entire room was rather dark and depressing, but at least it had a bed and was a warm place to sleep.

Camille strolled to the far side of the room and opened a door, revealing the en suite bathroom. "You'll have your own bathroom for tonight too."

"Thanks, Camille. This is great," Vincent said, appraising the room.

Camille shut the bathroom door and leaned her back against it, smiling prettily at Vincent. She tucked her reddish hair behind her ear. "I hope I've been a gracious host."

Vincent smiled back at her. "Of course. You've been amazing."

Leah stepped forward, so Vincent wasn't directly in front of Camille anymore. She yawned exaggeratedly and patted her mouth with her hand.

"Aww, sweetie, let's get you into bed," Vincent said, finally realizing she was exhausted.

"Sounds good. Goodnight, Camille," Leah said pointedly, with a glance at the door that led to the main part of the cabin.

But Camille didn't take the hint, or she didn't want to leave Vincent.

"Wait. I haven't shown you where the towels and toiletries—" Camille said in a rush.

Leah interrupted her, "It's fine. We'll figure it out."

Camille's face turned stony, and her eyes narrowed at Leah. "All right then. Goodnight." She finally stalked out of the bedroom, and Leah slammed the door when she was gone.

"What was that all about?" Vincent rubbed his chin.

"What do you mean?" Leah said, playing dumb. She didn't want to get into it with Vincent right now. Besides, she hadn't been exaggerating her tiredness. She was exhausted. The trip, the stress of the storm, and being trapped inside had taken everything out of her.

Vincent stood in front of her, holding her hands in between his. "You know what I mean. You and Camille being weird—"

"It's nothing. I'm tired, Vince." Leah dropped her gaze to the plush, off-white carpet.

"No, tell me. What is it? Is something wrong?"

Leah squeezed Vincent's hands and quickly made eye contact so he wouldn't keep pestering her. "Everything's fine."

Vincent's eyes narrowed as he scrutinized her. "You sure? You would tell me if something was wrong, wouldn't you?"

"What could be going on?" Leah asked, widening her blue eyes slightly to appear more innocent.

She didn't want Vincent to think she was paranoid that he and Camille had something going on between them. Or that she suspected he would cheat on her if he were alone with Camille for more than a minute. Maybe she was being paranoid, like Ava and Noah had told her. Nothing could have happened. Besides, wasn't that creepy? Camille was probably in her thirties, and Vincent was barely eighteen.

Vincent pulled his hands away from hers. "Fine, just keep secrets from me, then."

"I'm not! You're the one with a secret!" Vincent's face paled, and he bit his lip noticeably. "Wh—what secret?"

Now Leah worried her suspicions were right. Vincent didn't seem like himself, and he was clearly hiding something. Oh God, what was going on?

"Did you and Camille—"

Vincent laughed harshly, throwing his hands up in the air. "What about Camille?"

"I just... I thought maybe you—"

"What the hell, Leah? You think I cheated?"

"No, I don't. I don't know."

If that wasn't what he had meant, then what was her boyfriend hiding from her? What secret had he kept from her all this time? And why hadn't he told her? Whatever it was, it had to be something terrible if he still refused to tell her the truth.

"I can't believe this. After all we've been through together. We've been together for two years! *I love you, Leah*! Have I ever done anything to make you think otherwise?"

"Besides you forcefully grabbing my arm in the cabin when you wanted to leave this morning, no. Not really." Leah rubbed the sore spot on her arm. She supposed it would remain sore for a few days. His grip had been tight, and she barely had any muscle on her arms. The skin was bruised where he had held onto it.

Vincent's face fell at her reminder. His voice lowered. "I'm so sorry, Leah. I—I don't know what came over me then. I was angry, and I reacted stupidly, but I never meant to hurt you. You know I would never purposely harm you. I didn't mean to."

"I know you wouldn't," was all she said. She sighed and avoided eye contact with him. She wasn't being childish, was she? He *was* acting weird.

"Look, I want to tell you everything. I don't want there to be any secrets between us, but you have to trust me when I say I can't tell you this. It will change how you see me."

"How can I trust you if you're keeping things from me, though?" Leah asked hesitantly. She didn't want to have this conversation. She didn't want to fight with him, but she needed to know the truth. What was he hiding from her?

"You can trust me. I love you." Vincent gently touched her chin and lifted her face to meet his.

"I love you too." She tried to think of how to rephrase the question differently to make him want to talk about it.

Vincent's lips landed on hers in a soft kiss. He deepened the kiss and pulled her close to him so his body was against hers. She wrapped her arms around him, passionately kissing him back.

"Time for bed," Leah said, stopping the kiss abruptly and lifting the blanket up so she could slide underneath and get comfortable.

She glanced over at Vincent to see him pouting. She rolled her eyes. He was so predictable. "We are so *not* having sex right now."

Leah gave him a perfunctory kiss on the lips and turned over, facing away from him to fall asleep. Vincent sighed loudly, but Leah ignored it, doing her best to shut off her racing thoughts so she could sleep.

Vincent's secret could wait until tomorrow. He clearly wasn't ready to give it up. But he wasn't cheating on her, and he loved her. She repeated the words in her mind like a mantra. Those were the important things. Besides, Vincent didn't know everything about her. Leah had secrets of her own.

Chapter 12:
Camille

Camille poured a fresh cup of coffee and settled the mug onto a coaster on her desk. It was her favorite mug—a ceramic one covered in pretty cherry blossom flowers. Robert had brought it back from Tokyo years ago, during one of his business trips.

A scented candle was lit, the flame flickering in the darkening room. The smell of coffee and the apple candle mingled in the air, creating a delicious aroma perfect for her writing atmosphere. The power was all hers to wield, held right at her fingertips. Her eyes locked on her typewriter—her beautiful, trusted instrument.

Brody was already asleep in his dog bed underneath her desk. He was unnaturally still, so she checked to make sure he was okay. She sat in her desk chair, scooted the chair closer to the desk, and straightened her posture, readying herself to write.

Brody snored lightly beside her feet. Steam curled up from the coffee mug as Camille sipped her drink, savoring the warmth and the jolt of caffeine. For a moment, she pondered what to do next until her fingers touched the letters on the typewriter. The keys shimmered as she typed, almost glowing as she wreaked havoc on her characters. Those poor things had no clue what was in store for them.

***

Camille turned over on the couch for the dozenth time that night. It wasn't the worst place she had slept. Years ago, she and Robert had stayed in hostels throughout Europe. She remembered sharing a double bed with a lumpy mattress barely big enough to fit the two of them. Several other people slept in the same room. But she had been younger then and much more equipped to handle adventuring and tackling the day with little sleep. Now she was nearing forty—not that she was old—but old enough that every night of restless sleep left her with new aches the next day. She couldn't bounce back like she used to. She tried to stretch out her legs into a more comfortable position, but Brody was lying across her feet, and she didn't want to wake him.

Wearily sighing, Camille sat up and rubbed her eyes, looking over at the clock on her desk across the room. She could barely make out the blurry, glowing red numbers in the darkness: 4:46 a.m. She had only slept for three hours. As she leaned against the arm of the couch, Brody raised his head to look at her, making sure she wasn't leaving him. He never wanted to miss out on anything.

Camille made herself get up and walked to the large picture window near the front door. She pushed aside the large red-and-white checkered curtains to see outside. The snow was gone, revealing the limp grass in her yard and her desolate garden. Her guests would leave today, and she would be alone again.

Padding lightly over to the kitchen, she took great care not to make much noise. She didn't want to wake anyone and disturb their assumed peace. It was better if they slept now, before things got worse for them.

Camille set down the coffeepot to brew a fresh pot. She hummed quietly to herself as the water in the coffee maker heated, emitting a hiss as it poured into the coffeepot. She made toast and spread a healthy amount of jam across the bread. Afterward, she set her plate of toast on the small table in the kitchen, then poured herself a generous cup of black coffee.

Today, she was using a different mug—one she had bought at a souvenir shop in Paris during her backpacking trip with Robert. It was a cheap mug from one of those peddlers selling Paris-themed souvenirs on the streets, but it had held up for quite a while. The image of the Eiffel Tower painted on the side of the mug had faded with use, so only a faint outline remained.

As she pulled out one of the kitchen chairs with a disturbing screeching sound, Brody trotted into the kitchen to join her. He sat patiently, waiting under the kitchen table, looking up at her expectantly. She sat in the chair and broke off a tiny piece of toast without jam, then threw it under the table to him.

While eating breakfast and enjoying her coffee, Camille couldn't help but miss Robert. They had spent so many mornings like this together. Some mornings they drank their coffee in silence, but it was never an uncomfortable silence, not in the presence of the man she loved.

Other mornings, they had chatted about their plans for the weekend, future trip ideas, things to fix around the house, what to cook for dinner, a new movie coming out—whatever was on their minds.

Camille hadn't hidden any part of herself from Robert until he forced her to. But she didn't want to think about that. She didn't want to spoil her mood this morning. It would ruin the entire day if she dwelled on what had happened between them.

Camille finished her breakfast, washed off the plate, and refilled her empty coffee mug. Some days required more coffee than others, and today was an extra coffee type of day, especially since she hadn't gotten enough rest during the night.

On the bright side, she felt good about the words she had added to her book. Her latest book was coming along nicely—better than the previous one. That one went in the trash. Her agent hadn't liked it much and had suggested she try something different. After all the hard work Camille had put into it, the months of writing and re-writing, devastation overcame her. It was always difficult to let go of a story she was invested in. But she was determined for her next novel to be fantastic. A real page-turner.

Camille set the coffeepot down and headed into the main room of the cabin with her full mug of coffee. She placed the mug on a crocheted coaster on the coffee table—she despised stains and kept her cabin nearly immaculate all the time—and set about building a fire in the fireplace. Once the fire burned steadily, she pulled her quilt off the couch and wrapped it around her shoulders, sitting in front of the fireplace and sipping her coffee in contentment. Brody sprawled out in front of the fireplace. Camille nudged him back a bit, so he wasn't too close to the fire. He always tried to get too close when he was cold, and she worried about him catching on fire.

At some point, Camille must have dozed off because when she came to, someone tapped her shoulder and startled her awake. She whipped around, anxious about who was in the cabin, forgetting momentarily that four guests were staying with her.

Vincent stared back at her with a wry smile. "Good morning," he said cheerfully. "Sorry to scare you. Do you mind if we have some coffee before we head out?"

"Of course." Camille stood abruptly, letting the quilt fall to the floor. Her coffee mug was empty, so she picked it up and brought it back into the kitchen to refill it. *Well, a lot of good that caffeine did.*

Camille moved to scoop more coffee grounds into the coffee maker, but Vincent's hand was already on the scoop. He pulled back, and Camille's face warmed as their hands brushed.

"Oh, uh, sorry," he stuttered. "I can do it."

"It's fine. I don't mind."

"The others are still sleeping." Vincent relinquished his hold on the scoop and headed to the kitchen table.

"I'll brew a full pot, anyway. They'll probably want some before the long trip."

Vincent nodded and sat down while the coffee brewed. "Thanks again for... well, everything. I don't know what we would have done if we didn't have a place to shelter the past two nights. I don't think we would have survived in the woods because of how cold it's been. The snowstorm has been brutal."

Camille sat across from Vincent at the table and folded her hands in front of her. "It's been a pleasure having you stay with me. I only wish I could have gotten to know you better. You remind me so much of..." she trailed off, not finishing her sentence.

"Who? Your husband?"

Camille nodded wordlessly.

"What's he like? You said he's in Tokyo on business?" Vincent asked with apparent interest.

"Yes, he travels quite a bit for work. I miss him fiercely when we're apart."

"Since you're a writer... I don't want to sound rude or anything, but why don't you go with him when he travels? Can't you write anywhere?"

Camille's face tightened, and she gritted her teeth. "I wouldn't be able to. The typewriter is a pain to travel with, and I prefer it to using a pen and paper. And now, with Brody, I don't relish the thought of leaving him at the kennel for so long. It's difficult to travel with a dog."

"Oh yeah, that makes it harder when you have a pet. He seems like a good dog, though." Vincent eyed the dog sitting near his feet underneath the table.

"Yes, he's splendid company. I'm much better off with him around.

Not as lonely with Robert gone."

"When will he be back?"

Camille's eyebrows scrunched together as she thought. "I—I can't remember. I think he said April twenty-seventh."

Vincent frowned. "That can't be right. Today is the twenty-seventh."

"No, I—I meant he'll be home then. Not here at the cabin. This is just our getaway place. Our second home."

"Oh. How much longer are you staying here? I'm sure you want to get home and see him."

The coffee maker beeped, and Camille hurriedly stood to get coffee for Vincent. She grabbed a mug and poured coffee into it, laughing nervously.

"My goodness, you have a lot of questions! So curious."

"Sorry, just making conversation," Vincent said as Camille set the coffee mug in front of him.

"No, it's—it's fine. I'm not used to talking much about myself anymore. I suppose I forget how to talk to people sometimes. It's been nice having you here." Camille smiled.

Vincent returned the smile, and they lapsed into silence. Camille enjoyed the warmth and comfort of the coffee and his presence. She only hoped he felt the same.

"To be honest, I'm kind of dreading going home," Vincent spoke, shattering the silence after a few minutes had passed.

"Oh, why is that?"

"My dad was the only family member I had left. With him gone now, I don't know what I'll do. Before he died, I had a plan. Move out, go to college, marry Leah... It all seems so pointless." Vincent sipped his coffee, then abruptly put the mug down. "I didn't mean the part about marrying Leah! I just don't know what to do without my dad."

"That sounds very difficult. I'm sure it changed how you think about things. And I'm sure losing him in such a horrific way didn't help,"

Camille responded.

Vincent stared at her for a few seconds and pursed his lips. "How did you know? I didn't tell you that he committed suicide."

"Well, I assumed it was that or something else terrible. People rarely want to talk about such things," she said carefully.

She held her coffee mug up to her lips, taking a sip of the steaming liquid and hoping her face gave nothing away.

Chapter 13: Leah

Leah reached out her arm, expecting to find Vincent's warm body next to hers, ready for a cozy morning cuddle. However, her arm went through the air and landed on the cotton sheets. He wasn't there. Her eyes snapped open. *Where is Vincent?*

Leah's gaze traveled around the room, searching for her boyfriend. The bathroom door stood ajar, so she clambered out of bed and peeked inside the en suite. No sign of him. She sighed, now in a grumpy mood. He was probably hanging out with Camille.

She quickly changed out of her pajamas and into the outfit she had worn yesterday. Re-wearing clothes would have to do for now. It's not like she packed all of her outfits for their hike three days ago. Luckily, she'd had some spare clothes with her.

Once she was wearing her athletic leggings and long-sleeved shirt, she entered the bathroom to brush her hair and teeth. Satisfied with her appearance, she left the bedroom to find Vincent. He wasn't in the main room of the cabin, so she continued to the kitchen. He was sitting at the kitchen table across from Camille, and they were both laughing.

With a forced grin, Leah approached Vincent with fake cheerfulness, not wanting to upset him if he was in a good mood. "Morning," she greeted him. She sat on his lap and kissed him, placing her hands on either side of his face to prolong the kiss.

"Whoa. Morning, sweetie," Vincent replied with a huge grin cracking across his face.

"How'd you sleep?" Leah asked. She playfully tugged on Vincent's ponytail, then stood and stepped away, leaving him to look at her longingly. She knew exactly what she was doing with him. Plus, she knew he loved how her legs and butt looked in this pair of leggings.

"Great. What about you?"

"Me too." Leah turned to Camille. "The bed was so comfy. I hope the couch was all right."

Camille grimaced and raked a hand through her hair. "It was fine. It was worth losing a night of sleep to get some words in. I stayed up late anyway, so it's not like I had much of a chance to sleep."

"Oh," Leah said, shifting on her feet. "Well, we'll be leaving soon, so you'll have your place back!"

Camille took a sip of her coffee and set the mug back on the table with a loud bang. "Don't worry about it."

Leah helped herself to some coffee. She needed to wake up more, so she could be alert for the hike back to their campsite. They had a long day ahead of them, not only because of the hike back to the tent, but they still had to pack up their campsite and start the drive back home.

By the time Leah had finished her coffee, and Vincent and Camille had finished theirs—who knew how many cups those two drank before she was awake—Ava and Noah stumbled out of the spare bedroom. Ava's hair was matted to her head, and Noah's short, spiky blond hair stuck up all over. He brushed his hand through it futilely, not making it look much better. Ava and Noah both grumbled something that sounded like 'good morning' and raced to the coffeepot, fighting over who poured the first cup.

Vincent and Camille gave up their seats for Ava and Noah, while Leah went over to the fireplace to warm up. Brody was lying in front of the fire, happily warming himself. When he noticed Leah, he rolled onto his back, exposing his stomach. Leah laughed and scratched his belly, and his tail thumped obnoxiously against the wood floor.

Soon, Camille and Vincent came into the room as well. Vincent sat on the couch, and Camille seemed to hesitate before sitting in the armchair closest to the fireplace.

"So, back to Michigan soon. How long of a drive is it?" Camille asked politely.

"About ten and a half hours if traffic isn't too bad," Vincent replied. "We live in Grand Rapids. We'll have to stop a few times for food and bathroom breaks and to fill up the van with gas, though, so it will take longer."

"Yeah, we'll probably be home tomorrow." Leah glanced at Vincent for confirmation.

"Hopefully. As long as we don't have any other incidents." Vincent's lips pressed tightly together.

"I hope you have a safe drive home. It's been lovely having some company these last few days. It was a pleasant break from the solitude," Camille said graciously.

"Thank you. We appreciate everything," Leah said before Vincent could reply.

"Do you need any snacks or anything for the road?" Camille asked.

"No, we should be fine. We still have some food in the van, so we can eat that during the drive home," Vincent said.

"Are you sure? I don't mind giving you a few things to eat," Camille offered. "I still have an adequate amount of food here for myself."

"No, really, *you've done enough*," Leah said, the tone coming out ruder than she had intended.

Camille giggled in a high-pitched tone. "All righty then."

Vincent's and Leah's bags sat waiting by the door, like when they had tried to leave the previous morning. As usual, they were waiting for Noah and Ava. Leah thought this would be the last trip Vincent would ever take with them. Between Ava whining about the bathroom situation while camping, plus the food choices and the cold, and Noah complaining about the lack of video games and technology and how much his legs hurt from hiking, Vincent wouldn't forget how they had made the trip harder on him. The trip was supposed to take his mind off of things, not stress him out and anger him even more.

"I don't feel well," Vincent blurted out, making eye contact with Leah for help.

She looked him over. His face seemed paler than usual, and sweat glistened on his face in the fire's light. She pressed the back of her hand to his forehead.

"You feel warm, sweetie. What's wrong?"

"I'm not sure. I think I might throw up." Vincent closed his eyes and leaned back into the couch with a grimace.

"Oh no! Want me to help you to the bathroom?"

"No." He paused. "I don't know."

"Hold on a sec. I'll get you some water."

Leah went into the kitchen, opened a few of the cupboards until she found a cup, then filled it with water and brought it to Vincent.

He took the cup from her and gulped the water down greedily. He sighed and wiped his mouth with his sleeve.

"Better?" she asked, appraising him with concern. She touched his arm gently.

Vincent shrugged, his face still looking pale. "Not really. I think I might go lie down for a while."

Leah frowned, thinking over the situation and wondering what could have caused Vincent to suddenly feel sick. No one else was sick, just Vincent. She glanced toward the kitchen. "Have you eaten anything today?"

"I just had a cup of coffee and some eggs Camille made for me earlier."

The thought crossed her mind that Camille may have done something to his food. She immediately dismissed the thought. *No, Camille wouldn't do that.* She had been nice to them, helped them, and offered her cabin to them so they could shelter from the snowstorm. She wasn't that type of person.

Then what was it? Food poisoning?

"Did the eggs taste weird or look like they were undercooked?" she asked.

"I don't remember. They tasted fine. They looked like eggs."

Leah sighed. That was no help. Vincent wasn't feeling well, though, so she would take care of him, the way he always took care of her.

An hour later, Ava pranced out of the bathroom, more dolled up than anyone going on a three-mile hike ever had been. They were ready to leave at last.

Vincent claimed he was fine to travel, despite seeming unwell still, so they said their goodbyes to Camille, thanked her for everything she had done for them, and set off to find their campsite.

This time, when Vincent opened the front door, there wasn't much snow outside. It was melting, and the yard was full of slushy piles. The path appeared mostly clear, visibility was high, and the sun was shining—all good signs for a pleasant hike.

Once they were outside with their backpacks on and ready to go, Leah turned back toward the cabin. Camille waved and smiled in a way that made Leah wonder what was going through the writer's mind. What did it mean? She raised her shoulders toward her ears and then lowered them, trying to let the tension out of her body. It didn't matter. They were out of the cabin, and they wouldn't have to see Camille ever again.

Chapter 14: Camille

The four teenagers left her cabin and headed down the path that supposedly led back to their campsite. Leah turned around and looked back at her with a strange expression on her face, so Camille waved and smiled in what she thought was a friendly manner. She shut the door and entered her cabin to a desolate silence.

Over the past three days, she had gotten used to having them around. After months of solitude, besides Brody, she had adjusted to the constant presence of Noah's booming laugh, Ava's high-pitched voice and playful attitude, Leah's practical demeanor, and Vincent's gorgeous, dark hair, his warm, chocolate-brown eyes, and his—well, it was best not to dwell on him.

She supposed she would miss them since they were gone. Unless she did something about it.

No, that would be silly. They were gone now, and it was best to go back to her old life, working on her novel in solitude, with Brody as her only company. It had been a stupid idea, anyway. She could finish writing the novel in a few weeks if she hunkered down and pushed herself, then she could go home.

She would feel better once she was home, she decided. Maybe then she could pick up the pieces of her life again. She shuddered, thinking about what was waiting for her at her main house.

With no distractions preventing Camille from her work, she sat down at her desk with yet another mug of coffee on the crocheted coaster. She had lost track of how many cups of coffee she had drank today. She could always nap later if she was too tired. The cabin was all hers again, the way she preferred it. No one was around to judge her for taking a three-hour nap at 1:00 p.m. if she chose to do so. Or to disapprove if she baked brownies and ate them for breakfast. She could do as she pleased, and that was just fine with Camille.

Or, at least, that's what she tried to convince herself while she set about working on her novel again.

Camille wrote for several hours, typing furiously on her typewriter as the words thundered out of her. Sometimes writing was easy like this, and her fingers couldn't keep up with her brain.

Satisfied, she reread the last page she had typed, making sure it made sense. She didn't want to have issues with plot holes later on. Suddenly, exhaustion overcame her. As she stared at the typed page, her eyes became steadily heavier and began closing until she could hardly keep them open. She couldn't stop herself from drifting off at her desk and knew she should make herself get up and go to her bed. It wouldn't do to fall asleep at her desk. That would surely wreak havoc on her already aching body.

Weary with sleep, she got up and made it to her bed, then flopped facedown into her pillow, which held the faint, lingering smell of musk and coffee—Vincent's scent. She inhaled the smell, not wanting to wash her sheets and bedding, which would get rid of Vincent's presence. It was one of the few things she had left of him.

Brody whined until she let him hop up onto the bed with her. He settled next to her and stretched out his little paws, curling up beside her under the covers.

That afternoon, Camille dreamed of a group of four people hiking through Asheville, searching for their car. The blonde girl froze in her tracks, scared witless by the sound of an animal roaring close by. She clutched the hand of the brown-haired girl beside her and looked over at a man with short, blond hair, who seemed unsure of what to do.

A big, black bear ambled out of the woods toward the trail they were on with obvious intent. It had spotted them. The fourth member of the group—a tall man with long, dark hair in a ponytail—took charge, telling the others what to do.

Camille wondered what would happen to them. Would the bear attack or would they be able to scare it away? How were you supposed to react to a bear walking by you if you didn't have a gun or a way to defend yourself? These weren't normal things people learned in school or were taught by their parents.

It was as if Camille was God, looking down on them and observing their actions, judging them for every wrong decision they made and applauding every correct choice. The feeling filled her until she sizzled with power, making her want more.

She turned over restlessly in her sleep, her eyes wildly fluttering open as an enormous crash came from somewhere outside her bedroom, and cacophony ensued.

Chapter 15: Leah

Ava's nails dug into Leah's arm. She clung to her sister. The bear roared. It lazily ambled toward them. Ava screamed, and Leah tried to shush her. Screaming wouldn't help their predicament. Leah racked her brain. She knew little about encountering bears. Hunting and camping had never been her forte. Her head whipped around, searching for Vincent. He'd been camping with his dad a lot. He would know what to do. Right?

She locked her wide-eyed stare on him.

Vincent staggered forward. He held out his arms. Slowly, he reached a shaking hand into his bag. He pulled out a canister. Leah realized it was bear repellant.

She let out a long exhale. Relief flooded through her. Vincent was always prepared for any situation.

"I'm going to scare it away," Vincent told them, his voice unusually high-pitched. "Keep your distance."

Vincent slowly raised his arms above his head. He jumped and let out a powerful, ringing blow that rattled in Leah's ears. She resisted the urge to cover them with her shaking hands. Not only was she trapped in Ava's tight grip, but she was frozen solid with fear.

Vincent paused his movements, and Leah worried things were about to take a turn for the worst. Why wasn't he moving? Was the bear about to attack?

Oh, God. Please, no. Her breath hitched in her chest.

Vincent waited a moment, then leaped into the air again and screamed. Swiftly, he reached down and snatched up handfuls of pine needles and sticks from the trail at his feet, then hurled them at the beast.

The bear watched them for a moment and continued its pursuit of them.

"It's not working!" Ava screeched.

"Start walking down the trail." Vincent held the bear repellant in his right hand, pointing it at the bear.

Leah knew bear repellant was basically a super strong version of pepper spray, but it should be sufficient to temporarily blind the bear, so they could get away safely.

"On the count of three, I'm going to spray the bear, and we'll continue down the trail. Okay?" Vincent commanded.

Everyone nodded and prepared themselves to escape.

"Okay. One... Two... Three!" Vincent shot forward, aiming for the bear's face and expelling the bear repellant with a hiss.

The bear emitted a loud howling sound. It swiped at its eyes, halting in its tracks. Immediately, Leah turned and ran down the trail. Ava and Noah followed close behind her. Vincent remained at the back of the group. For a quarter mile, they moved at a fast pace. Vincent caught up and called for them to stop.

Vincent held his hand against his abdomen as if he was in pain. "The bear is probably regaining its vision by now, but we should be far enough away that it either won't be able to find us or it will have gone somewhere else to look for food. I'm sure there are other campsites and cabins nearby. Bear repellent is like pepper spray. It should inflame their eyes and upper respiratory system," Vincent said. "We can slow down for a bit."

"Are you sure?" Ava's lip trembled as she slowed down, but she kept moving down the trail. "That was terrifying. I thought we were going to die!" Tears quivered on her pretty, long lashes.

Leah hugged her sister, making her stop in her tracks. "It's okay. We're safe now," Leah reassured Ava.

"Holy shit," Noah exclaimed. He turned to Vincent. "Good thing you had that bear repellant! Although, I totally could have taken that bear if it had charged at us." He held up his fists in a mock fighting stance.

A smile graced Ava's face as she swiped Noah's hands down.

Vincent rolled his eyes good-naturedly at Noah's antics.

"Sure, dude," Vincent said. "That's why you looked like you were about to piss yourself and just stood there, while I tried everything I could think of so we could get away. Even though I'm the one who's feeling sick, I still saved all of our asses."

Leah laughed. "I'm just glad we're all right. I want to get back to the campsite. How much further is it?"

They all halted on the trail so Vincent could check the map again.

Once he pinpointed their location, he traced a finger across the path. "About a mile and a half more. We're a little over halfway there. Shouldn't be too much longer."

"Right. Let's get going. I think I'll feel better once we're in the van and on our way home," Leah said, adjusting her bag on her shoulders.

Vincent moved to the front of the group and set off. Holding his map in front of his body and checking it every so often, he led them the rest of the way to the campsite. Because of the rough terrain, it took around forty-five minutes before they spotted their campsite.

Tears pricked Leah's eyes when she saw the familiar dark blue tent was still intact, despite the crazy weather and unexpected snowstorm. Before their hike, they had packed all their camping supplies into the bear canister to prevent bears from being attracted to their campsite. Thankfully, their supplies remained untouched.

Ava unzipped the tent and started packing up their sleeping bags, pillows, and other items they had left in the tent. Leah assisted her while the guys gathered their food from the bear canister. They took down the tent and packed it away, then loaded up the van, which was parked nearby.

Three hours after they had left Camille's cabin, they had stuffed the van with their belongings.

"Just gotta take a piss first," Noah said as he wandered into the woods, far enough away that no one could see him.

Leah grimaced at his crudeness and opened the passenger door of the van, sliding into the passenger seat.

Vincent was waiting in the driver's seat already. "I'll drive first," he said. "You can drive next, then Noah, and last, Ava. If we switch off every few hours, everyone can rest. We should be home by tomorrow."

"Sounds like a plan. I want to find a pay phone when we're on the road, so Ava and I can call our parents. We should let them know what's going on and tell them we'll be home tomorrow."

"Good idea. Then someone will know our whereabouts in case something happens," Vincent replied.

"What do you—" Leah said as Noah slid open the back door of the van and climbed into the back seat.

Ava opened the door on the other side and sat next to Noah. "Ready?" Ava asked.

"Yup, all set," Vincent said. "I was just saying to Leah that she can drive next. The trip shouldn't be too bad if we all take a turn driving."

After Vincent had been driving for barely ten minutes, Noah and Ava had already both passed out in the back seats. Leah giggled when she noticed and commented to Vincent that those two could sleep through the world ending. She envied them for how easily they could fall asleep, but it was for the best if they rested.

"I'll drive until we get to Lexington. It's like four hours away. Do you mind taking over then? Let Ava and Noah sleep for now," Vincent suggested.

"Sure, that's fine. I can drive for a few hours, and if they aren't awake by then, we'll wake them up. I'm sure we'll all be hungry too."

Vincent turned on the radio and spun the dial until he found a heavy metal station. Ava and Noah somehow slept through the screams and guitar riffs.

At first, Vincent and Leah quietly chatted about the trip, about how lucky they had been several times—not only by finding Camille and safe shelter for three days, but also for narrowly escaping a bear attack—and both repeatedly mentioned that they couldn't wait to be home. After they had talked through everything, they fell into a comfortable silence.

As Vincent concentrated on driving and focused on the road, Leah occupied herself by staring out the window. The van wound down the steep mountainside, with mist seeming to settle around them, shielding them from the rest of the world. Trees nestled together across the cliffs, the branches naked and forlorn.

"What a crazy trip." Vincent shook his head as he drummed his fingers on the steering wheel. He turned the knob to switch the radio station to classic rock.

Leah laughed forcefully. "Crazy doesn't even begin to explain it."

"Hey, at least we made it to the van. We'll be home soon. The worst is over." Vincent took his eyes off the road for a second to glance at Leah. He smiled at her.

"Keep your eyes on the road!" she chided him.

"I'm fine. Calm down." Vincent focused on the road again.

Leah returned her gaze to the mountains, enjoying the reprieve from their stressful trip. They would be home later, and everything would be fine.

A moment later, a grinding noise started coming from the van. It became louder and more insistent as they continued driving.

As Leah wondered what it meant, the dashboard lit up with multiple warning signals. The signals flashed sporadically on and off.

Leah wiped her clammy hands on her leggings and made eye contact with Vincent. "Vince, something's wrong!" she yelled, pointing to the dashboard.

"Huh? Oh, shit," Vincent said, glancing down at the dashboard to see what she meant. "Hang on." He turned on the right turn signal and pulled the van onto the shoulder, then flipped the hazards on.

As Vincent drove the van onto the gravel shoulder, the bumpy drive and the sound of the tires crunching over gravel woke up Noah and Ava.

"What's going on?" Ava asked, holding her hand over her mouth to stifle a yawn.

"Something's wrong with the van." Leah unbuckled her seatbelt and turned around to face her sister and Noah in the back seat.

Vincent cut the engine, looked both ways, and jumped out of the van, popping open the hood to inspect the engine. Soon after Vincent left the car, Noah went outside too.

Ava snorted. "What do you even know about cars?" she called after him.

"The car was making a weird grinding noise," Leah said to Ava.

"Hmm, it's been fine for the whole trip," Ava replied.

"Maybe because it was left out in the cold and snow?" Leah suggested. "We haven't started it in a few days, so that could have something to do with it."

Ava shrugged and inspected her nails. "Yeah, maybe. I'm sure the guys will figure it out. Or Vincent will, I mean."

Ten minutes later, Vincent slammed the hood of the car and returned to his spot in the driver's seat. Noah climbed to his previous position in the back seat.

"What's wrong?" Leah asked, anxiously leaning toward Vincent the second he was back in the car.

He shook his head. "I'm not sure. Everything looks fine, but neither of us is a mechanic, so—"

"So, you don't know what to look for," Ava finished with a sigh.

"Well, I know the basic stuff to check," Noah protested.

Ava turned to him. With a huff, she said, "Yeah? Like what, Mr. Car Expert?"

Noah grumbled to himself, but he didn't answer audibly.

"I'll get us onto the main road and find a service station. I'm sure there's one nearby. We can have someone check out the van before we get too far away. I wouldn't want to get stuck in the middle of nowhere," Vincent said.

Vincent turned the keys in the ignition, muttering as he did so. The van made a sputtering noise, but nothing happened.

Leah clasped her hands together, hoping the van would miraculously be fine.

Vincent took out the keys, re-inserted them, and tried starting the engine again. The dashboard lit up with multiple warning signals again, but the engine wouldn't turn over. The van wouldn't start.

"Fuck!" Vincent exclaimed, slamming his hand against the steering wheel and accidentally honking the horn.

"What are we going to do?" Ava said, her hands clutching the back of Leah's headrest.

Vincent smacked his hand against the steering wheel again. "We don't know where the closest service station is, but we aren't too far from Camille's cabin..."

Ava groaned and raised her shoulders to her ears. "No! I don't want to go back there. I want to go home."

"Ava, I don't think we have a choice. If the van won't start, then it's probably best to leave it here and go back to Camille's place," Leah said.

"How will we get home, then?" Noah asked. "Call a tow truck at Camille's?"

Vincent nodded. "Yeah, that's what I was thinking. I'm sure she has a phone. We can ask a mechanic to tow the van and fix it. We'll be home in no time. This is just a minor detour."

"A detour on the trip from hell," Ava muttered as she laid her head back against the head rest.

"Fine, let's get going, then." Leah ignored her sister's comment. She resigned herself to heading back to Camille's cabin. If the van wouldn't start, there was nothing around for miles, and they had no way of calling for help, not only was it their best option, but it seemed like their only option.

Chapter 16: Camille

Hurriedly, Camille clambered out of bed to see what all the ruckus was about. Brody followed her, barking at the sudden onslaught of noise in the formerly silent cabin. She tentatively opened her bedroom door and said, "Hello?"

No one was there.

She moved into the main room of the cabin and heard pounding on the door. *Ah, of course. Visitors.*

She opened the front door to reveal Leah, Vincent, Ava, and Noah standing outside. Her house guests were back.

When Camille spotted their distraught faces, she nearly burst into gleeful laughter. It was good to be the one in control. This was what she was meant for. She deserved this... this gift. It was glorious to be the one with all the power.

Brody ran up to them and barked at the intruders.

Camille allowed herself a small smile, careful to appear out of the loop. She pressed her hand to her chest, clutching her red and black flannel shirt in faux surprise. "Oh my goodness! What on earth are you all doing back here?"

Vincent was the first one to speak up. "We made it back to our campsite and found the van, but... well... Is it okay if we come inside to explain what happened?" Vincent asked, peeking into the cabin and frowning.

"We—we were driving through the—the mountains, and the engine stalled—" Leah explained at the same time as Vincent, stumbling over her words.

"Come inside and tell me what happened. I sense a story brewing." Camille opened the front door widely and ushered them back into her cabin.

They all entered and made themselves at home on the couch once again.

Camille smirked. This was fun. She wondered what they would come up with. How would they explain what had happened? "I can make some coffee while we sort things out," she offered, ever the gracious hostess.

"Okay, yeah, sounds good," Vincent said.

Ten minutes later, Camille returned, her arms full with the coffeepot and mugs. Vincent jumped up to help her set everything on the coffee table. He was such a gentleman. She poured coffee for each of them, offered them cream and sugar, then settled into her usual place in her oversized plaid armchair. She observed the teenagers as they tried to explain what had happened.

"So, we were driving through the mountains, and a bunch of warning signals lit up on the dashboard. I pulled over onto the shoulder and turned off the van to check out what was going on. I popped the hood, and Noah and I looked things over." Vincent hesitated, as if he was choosing his words carefully. "Neither of us knows much about cars, so we weren't able to figure out what was wrong. We planned to look for a service station, but when I tried starting the van again, the engine wouldn't turn over. I'm assuming the battery is dead. Since we weren't too far from your cabin, we figured our best option was to walk back here and borrow your phone to call a tow truck," Vincent explained.

"Oh, my goodness! Well, that sounds like a doozy, but we'll leave that to the mechanics, won't we?" Camille waved her hand toward the kitchen. "There's a phone in there with a phone book in the drawer next to the fridge. You can call a tow truck and wait here until they arrive. At least you'll be warm and safe while you wait."

"Thank God," Ava said, reaching for Noah's hands. "We were worried you wouldn't have a phone."

"Oh, I don't think many people get by without a phone nowadays. It's necessary, especially living out here by myself," Camille said with a small smile.

Vincent went into the kitchen to flip through the phone book and find a towing company. They heard him chatting for several minutes before he returned.

"Well?" Leah said impatiently, standing when he came back.

"They're not super busy since it's a weekday, so they said they would be here in an hour at the most. Their garage is about twenty miles away. If it's just the battery, then they should be able to replace it today," Vincent explained.

"So, we just have to wait here for an hour, and they'll come get us?" Ava asked, leaning against Noah.

"Yup, that's what the guy on the phone said," Vincent replied.

"What are we going to do for the next hour, then?" Ava asked, most likely already bored from sitting around in the cabin again.

"Just chill," Noah suggested. "We still have a long drive home today. Maybe we should take a nap." He yawned and stretched his arms up, then folded them behind his head.

Vincent shook his head. "Or we could help Camille with a few things around the cabin while we're here. She's been so nice to us, letting us stay here, offering us her food and a safe place to shelter from the storm. Plus, now she's letting us stay inside until the tow truck comes."

Camille's eyes brightened at the suggestion. "If you don't mind, there are a few things I could use some assistance with. It's a small cabin, and I'm no stranger to hard work, but I would appreciate the help. Sometimes it's a bit much to maintain everything, especially when my husband is gone."

"Sure." Vincent stood and slapped his hands against his knees. "What can we do?"

Noah stood with a sigh. He ran his hands through his short, blond hair. "Fine. If Vince is helping, then I will too. I can't have him make me look bad." He shot a grin at Ava, who merely smirked at him.

Camille brought them outside, while Leah and Ava waited in the sitting room. She showed Vincent and Noah the compost pile, and they helped her carry all the garbage outside. Then she brought them to the trees, where she usually gathered kindling and chopped firewood.

By the time they were done with the chores, an hour had passed, so they went back inside the cabin.

"Did the phone ring while we were gone?" Vincent asked, his eyes darting to Leah expectantly.

"No." Leah shook her head. "You didn't see the tow truck pull up?"

Vincent tilted his head to the side. "I wouldn't have asked if they called if they were here."

"Maybe something else came up? Let's just keep waiting," Leah said with a shrug.

"It's not like we have a choice!" Ava slapped her hand down on the arm rest of the couch.

"Hey, at least we're warm inside the cabin and not waiting on the side of the road, out in the cold. It could be worse, Ava," Leah chided her sister.

Ava let out a heavy sigh. "Okay, you're right, but that doesn't mean I like this. I want to go home, take a hot shower, put on some clean clothes, and sleep in my bed."

"Yeah, that sounds great," Noah agreed.

"You're welcome to take a shower in the guest bathroom while you're here, if you would like to," Camille offered.

"No, that's okay. We don't know when the towing company will show up, and we don't want to make them wait when they arrive," Leah said. "We'll shower when we get home tomorrow."

"Hopefully, they show up soon," Camille said.

Camille sipped her coffee, enjoying the warmth that flooded through her body—not just from the coffee, but from manipulating the situation without her house guests being aware of it. "It would be a shame if they were delayed."

Chapter 17: Leah

Two hours later, the phone still hadn't rung, and the towing company hadn't shown up, despite each of them intermittently peeking out the window and going outside to check for it.

Assuming the worst, Leah hesitantly spoke up, "What if something happened to the tow truck? The roads seemed slippery, and driving in the mountains can be dangerous. There aren't any guardrails for most of the Blue Ridge Parkway. It would be easy to accidentally drive off the side of the mountain if you were driving too fast—"

"I'm sure whoever drives the tow truck is an excellent driver. They would have to be in their line of work," Vincent said dismissively, waving his hand at Leah as if swatting away a fly. "But you might be right that something happened. I'll head down the road and check to see if anyone is there. They could have been delayed."

"What? No, you can't leave by yourself! Besides, what if they arrive and you're gone?" Leah's legs shook as she stood.

"Fine, then you can come with me. Noah and Ava can stay here in case the tow truck comes," Vincent ordered.

"Ugh, fine!" Ava crossed her arms over her chest and sank into the couch cushions.

Leah narrowed her blue eyes at her sister. "Are you really complaining about staying here? Because if you and Noah would rather be the ones who go out and walk potentially several miles in the cold and wind to see if the towing company is close by—"

"No, no. It's fine. Noah and I will wait here," Ava said quickly, sitting up straighter.

"Good luck," Noah called from the couch. He settled in and shut his eyes, looking like he was about to fall asleep.

"Come on, let's get going." Vincent placed his hand on Leah's, and they headed to the front door. "We'll be back soon."

Noah snored, and Ava waved halfheartedly.

Camille said, "Goodbye! I hope you find them."

Soon, they were outside again, heading down the trail toward the main road, hand in hand. They trudged through the dead grass and crunchy leaves. Once they reached the main road, Vincent made Leah walk on the side furthest from the cars driving by, so she was safer.

According to Vincent's rough estimate, they had barely made it a quarter of a mile down the main road when they saw something that made Leah stop dead in her tracks. She froze, staring at the ghastly sight and not quite believing that what she saw was real.

Vincent dropped her hand and ran toward the sight. A tow truck with "Smith's Towing" in bold, black letters on the side of it was flipped upside down on the opposite side of the road from where it should have been if it was headed toward Camille's cabin. The front end of the truck had smashed into a massive oak tree. Smoke still trailed from the hood of the truck, so the accident hadn't happened long ago.

An unsettling feeling came over Leah. A chill shuddered down her spine, and she wrapped her arms around herself. No one was standing outside of the truck, so unless they had already fled the scene, it didn't look good.

Vincent stepped closer to the truck and peered inside. "Hello?" he yelled, surveying the surrounding area. He examined the oak tree and the front of the truck. "Shit. Stay back."

"What is it, Vince?" she screamed, running to the truck to see what he had found. "Oh my God." Leah covered her mouth with both hands in horror at the sight a few feet away from the oak tree.

The driver had been an overweight man wearing overalls and scuffed-up, well-worn black boots. He was nearly bald, but he possessed a few stubborn, dark brown tufts on top of his head. His trucker hat was laying beside the truck, and it was in the best condition of anything at the accident scene. Blood sprayed across his overalls. Fragments of glass covered his face and arms. He wasn't moving.

Leah turned back to the tow truck and realized the windshield had an enormous hole in it. She hadn't noticed it in her hurry to find out what had happened.

"He must have lost control of the truck and hit the tree. If he was driving fast, then the impact of the truck hitting the tree would have sent him flying out," Vincent said in an analytical tone, echoing her thoughts. "He probably died quickly, at least."

"He's dead?" Leah gasped, avoiding looking at the poor man again and instead focusing her attention on Vincent. Tears sprang to her eyes as it sank in. This man had driven all the way here to tow their van to safety, fix their car issues, and help them get home, and now he was dead?

Vincent calmly went over to the driver, bent down, checked for a pulse, and stood back up. "I guess we should head back to Camille's house, then." He turned and headed back in the direction they had just come from.

Silently, Leah followed him, reflecting on the fact that on the walk here, they had been chattering away, full of hope and optimism about the prospect of going home, seeing their families soon, and sleeping in their own comfy beds again. But now, after the gruesome discovery of the dead man who had been coming to help them, they trudged back to the cabin without speaking.

Leah couldn't shake the feeling that something was very wrong with Vincent. He seemed cold and uncaring about the poor truck driver. Was he just trying to act tough for her sake, or was this proof that he wasn't the man she had fallen in love with anymore?

***

When they returned to the cabin, Leah dreaded telling Ava and Noah what they had found. What were they supposed to do? Sure, they could call the towing company and tell them what they thought had happened, but then what? Should they call another tow truck? Was there even another one close by? They were in the mountains of Asheville, and there weren't many businesses near enough who would drive out this way. Any other towing companies would probably charge a higher fee to drive further.

Leah and Ava's parents had given them a credit card for emergencies, and Leah supposed this was an emergency. Maybe their parents would be all right with them charging the extra fee if they didn't have another option.

As Leah pondered the situation, she couldn't stop the thought that it may not have been an accident from entering her mind. It was chilly and windy, but the sky was clear, and it was otherwise a perfect early spring day. What had made the driver lose control? Were there other forces at work in this town?

Leah let Vincent explain to everyone what they saw. Ava's and Noah's faces dropped in disappointment at being stuck in the cabin yet again. Camille offered to make everyone hot chocolate and came back into the sitting room with mugs for everyone.

Hesitantly, Leah voiced her opinion that something strange was happening—something preventing them from leaving the area and returning home. Vincent outright laughed at her, skeptical as always about anything otherworldly or magical. Surprisingly, Noah seemed to agree with her right away.

Leah picked up one of the coffee mugs and took a careful sip of hot chocolate. Steam curled up from the mug as she blew on it.

Noah threw up his hands agitatedly as he ranted, "Like we're in a sci-fi movie, or there's fucking magic involved! It's like we can't leave the cabin or something."

"Excuse me," Camille interrupted, clutching a coffee mug tightly in her hands, her knuckles turning white. "Please, no swearing in my house."

"Sorry," Noah said instantly. "I forgot about that. I'm just so worked up from the situation. What's going on? Something is keeping us from leaving. How are we supposed to get home?"

The four guests in Camille's cabin all stared at each other and then around the cabin as if searching for a hidden clue as to what had happened.

"Maybe there isn't a logical explanation," Camille offered. "Maybe you're back here for a reason, and you weren't supposed to go home yet."

They all turned to gawk at her, apparently bewildered by the idea.

"Our parents are going to be so worried when we don't come home tonight, like we promised," Leah said, biting her lip.

"Ugh, you're right. I can only imagine how much Mom is going to freak out when we don't show up. She'll probably call the cops and report us missing," Ava replied, putting her head in her hands.

"Yeah, my parents will be worried too," Noah said. "Our original departure date was today, right?"

"At least you have people back home to worry about you," Vincent said quietly as his shoulders drooped. He straightened his posture again as if he was trying to stuff down his sadness. "Anyway, we can use Camille's phone to call your parents. We'll let them know what happened and that we won't be home tonight."

Leah smiled sympathetically at her boyfriend, squeezing his hand. "You're right. It's not like we're trapped here. We left before, and we were on our way home. It wasn't until..." Leah trailed off as she pondered what had happened once again.

"What?" Vincent asked sharply, squeezing her hand back too hard. "What are you thinking?"

"Just that we had two near-death incidents today. The close call with the bear and then the car accident with the tow truck driver," Leah said, rubbing Vincent's hand absentmindedly and trying to make him loosen his grip. "I know we aren't sure of exactly what happened to the truck driver, but it's an awfully weird coincidence that we went out to look for the truck and found out the driver was dead."

"Hmm." Vincent's brow creased. He appeared thoughtful as he clasped Leah's fingers in his. "You're right. Plus, the van's battery died, or the alternator needs to be replaced. Almost as if we're being sabotaged."

"What are you guys saying? A magical force is working against us?" Ava laughed, but the sound came out as more of a screech, implying she was scared.

Noah snorted. "Yeah, some evil force is messing with us and doesn't want us to get home. That's a laugh."

"You're the one who suggested a sci-fi movie," Vincent said. "I hate to say I'm even entertaining this, but... what types of things happen in those sci-fi movies you watch? What's the one you're always obsessing over? *Alien?*"

Noah stared at Vincent, not blinking for a long moment. "You serious, dude? This isn't a sci-fi movie. It's real life. There aren't aliens in our world. That kind of stuff doesn't exist. And even if it did, why would someone or... or *something* not want us to get home? What would it want from us?"

Camille smiled primly, drinking her coffee and holding the cup to warm her chilled hands, even after she finished taking a sip. "There may be forces at work here that you were previously unaware of. Forces that are ancient and powerful." Her face darkened as she made eye contact with each of them. "I suggest not messing with those types of things and just letting it be."

"Wh-what do you mean 'letting it be?' So, we can't leave?" Ava's eyes welled with tears, and she buried her head in Noah's chest.

"We can't stay here forever. That would be crazy. We have lives back in Michigan, jobs, people who will miss us." Leah's expression mirrored Ava's.

"My recommendation is to wait it out," Camille told them with a firm nod.

"What's that supposed to mean?" Ava asked.

"Well, if there is an evil force or something magical interfering with your ability to get home, then it's safer if you stay here until you know what they want," Camille said.

Noah's voice was high-pitched as he asked, "What do they want from us?"

"Are we entertaining this now?" Vincent said, raising his eyebrows. "I was just playing devil's advocate. You guys don't really believe some evil force is messing with us, right?"

Leah nodded. "I think Camille might be right. At least we're safe in the cabin. Nothing can hurt us in here."

Camille's gaze dropped to her empty coffee mug, then her eyes flicked back to Leah. "Of course. Nothing can hurt you here," she said sweetly.

Chapter 18: Leah

Leah paced the main room of the cabin, which was now a familiar space. *At least there aren't bears in here, or windy mountain roads, or trees to crash into—nothing here that could kill us. We're safe*, she reasoned with herself.

But she couldn't fight the lingering feeling that evil lurked near them, waiting for an opportunity to strike.

Vincent touched her arm, trying to make her stop pacing. His warm, chocolate-brown eyes locked with hers. "Leah, sit down. We're going to be okay."

"Are we, though? We don't know what we're dealing with." She shook her head, her light brown hair fluttering around her thin shoulders.

"We're together, and that's what matters." Vincent clasped his hands over Leah's. "Together forever," he whispered, leaning forward until their foreheads lightly touched.

A small smile broke across Leah's face, and she gave Vincent a quick peck on the lips. "Forever," she whispered back.

"*Helloooo*. Attention, lovebirds." Ava waved her arms around wildly, interrupting their moment.

"Yeah?" Vincent said.

"How are we going to figure out who, or what, is interfering with us?" Ava asked, standing between them with her hands on her hips.

Leah thought for a minute. "I'm not sure," she answered honestly. "Any ideas?" Her gaze went to the others.

Vincent spoke up first. "We don't know for sure that some force or higher power is interfering. Honestly, that sounds even crazier when I say it out loud. I don't know what's going on, but we'll deal with it when we have to."

"What are we going to do, then?" Noah stood from the couch and tensed up, as if he was readying his body for a fight.

"We'll prepare. We don't have our camping supplies with us, which is unfortunate because I had a first aid kit and a lot of other things that could be helpful for many situations—"

"Get to the point, Vince," Noah cut him off, waving his hand in a 'hurry up' motion.

"Right. We can make sure we're ready for whatever's coming. We have no way to predict what will happen, but we sure as hell aren't going down without a fight." Vincent's voice raised as he spoke, and his tone was loud and determined by the time he stopped speaking.

Camille glared at him, presumably at his use of the word 'hell.'

Vincent quickly apologized.

"Sounds like a plan. What do we do first?" Noah asked, now pacing the small room as Leah had earlier.

Leah wondered if everyone else was as anxious as her. She would rather do something productive and make the most of their time, instead of sitting around worrying about what could happen next. What else could they do if they didn't yet know what they were up against?

"We need weapons and supplies," Vincent said, staring at Camille, who raised her eyebrows questioningly. "You're a woman living in a cabin alone in the woods. I assume you have some sort of weapon here to defend yourself," he said, not as a question, but as a statement.

"You're smart to think that, Vincent, but I'm not a violent person. Except maybe to the characters in my books. I don't own a gun," Camille added with a wicked grin. "I don't think I could kill a real person, even if an intruder broke in and tried to hurt me."

"Okay, so that idea's out. Where can we find weapons?" Noah asked, his gaze drifting to Vincent for advice. "It's not like there's a store close by that we can go to."

"We'll just have to make some, then." Vincent shrugged his shoulders as if it wasn't a big deal.

"*Make* some?" Ava repeated, her nose wrinkling in disgust. Whether her disgust was from the thought of having to work or specifically about making weapons, that remained to be seen.

"It'll be easy. My dad showed me how to—" Vincent stopped suddenly, his voice becoming strained. "I know how to make weapons. I can show you guys. Camille, do you have chili peppers and some sort of squirt bottle? Also, we need hairspray, a lighter, a rubber band, and some chocolate."

Camille nodded along as Vincent listed items until he said the word 'chocolate.' "What was that last one?" she inquired, tilting her head.

"The chocolate is just for us to snack on and to boost our moods." Vincent grinned.

Camille laughed unexpectedly. "I think I have some boxed brownies I can bake."

"Perfect," Vincent said.

Camille went into the kitchen to search for the brownies, and Leah immediately beckoned everyone to come closer to her.

"What is it, Leah?" Vincent asked, putting his arm around her.

The group of four huddled together, shoulders touching.

"Has anyone considered that Camille may be responsible for this?" Leah whispered.

"Whoa—what?" Noah said.

"Think about it! When we got lost during our hike, we found her cabin. The snowstorm came out of nowhere. Before we set off on our trip, we checked the weather forecast, and snow wasn't predicted this week. The snow lasted for days. When we thought the blizzard was over, it started up again. Then, when it was finally clear outside and safe to travel, we encountered a bear. When we were driving home, the van randomly died—"

"Are you trying to blame Camille for our bad luck because you're worried about her stealing Vincent away?" Noah chuckled.

Leah glared at him with venom in her eyes. "I told you not to tell him!"

Vincent's eyes widened, and he backed away from the group. "Wait—what? You're worried about me and Camille?" He laughed, then ran his hands through his ponytail and turned his head to look straight at his girlfriend. "You really think something happened between us, Leah?"

"No! I—I just thought—"

"That I cheated on you with some random woman who lives alone in a cabin in the middle of the woods?" Vincent shook his head again. "She's definitely not my type. Plus, she's way too old for me. You're the only one for me. Don't you know that?"

"Well, yes, but—" Leah said before Vincent cut her off again.

"Why are you being so insecure?" Vincent persisted.

"We can't talk about this right now. Everyone needs to hear me out about Camille and what she's been doing this whole time," Leah said. "I have a theory."

"I don't know, sis. It sounds crazy." Ava twirled her dyed blonde hair around her finger and then inspected it for split ends.

"Crazier than the fact that there could be an evil force tormenting us? Crazier than the fact that the van died with no sign that anything was wrong with it? Or that the driver of the tow truck had a deadly car accident when he was almost at the cabin?" Leah said with disdain, her voice rising with each question.

"Okay, granted, those are both examples of unfortunate things happening, but that wasn't Camille's fault." Vincent peered at each of them, daring someone to contradict him. "It's not like she's a... a witch."

Leah directed her gaze around the circle. "What do we know about her, besides the fact that she's a writer, she's supposedly married, and she has a dog named Brody? Hasn't anyone else noticed she barely talks about her personal life and always changes the subject when we ask what her book is about?"

"Maybe she doesn't enjoy talking about herself. Some people are weird like that," Ava said. "Plus, her life is kind of depressing. I mean, like, why does her husband keep traveling the world and leaving her alone in a cabin?"

"Exactly!" Leah exclaimed.

"What? Like you think she's not really married?" Noah asked. "Why would she lie about that?"

"I don't know! Why would she do any of this?" Leah asked impatiently, pressing her lips together. "The point is we need to find out the truth about Camille and—"

Camille came back into the room with a smile, which turned to a puzzled expression when everyone stopped talking.

They were still huddled closely together. Leah knew they looked suspicious.

"What were you all talking about?" Camille narrowed her eyes at them with the tray of brownies in her hands. Her knuckles turned white as she gripped the tray.

"Um..." Leah stuttered, trying to think of a plausible conversation topic that wouldn't be a dead giveaway.

"We're brainstorming a gift to thank you for your kindness. You've done so much for us, Camille, and we wanted to show you our appreciation," Ava explained quickly, with a radiant smile.

Leah shot her an approving glance. *Smart thinking, Ava.*

Camille seemed to like that answer, and her face glowed as she beamed. "Oh, that isn't necessary," she said with an airy hand gesture. "Goodness knows I don't need anything else to clutter up my cabin. Although, I would appreciate more firewood as the supply stashed inside is growing low."

Vincent and Noah both stepped up.

"We'll do that," Vincent offered. "No problem."

"Great. Be sure to only collect firewood from the trees I showed you earlier. No point in cutting down perfectly good living things and harming things we shouldn't. That would be irresponsible."

Chapter 19: Camille

After collecting more firewood, Camille and her guests gathered in the cabin, eating brownies and drinking mugs of freshly brewed coffee. Camille lounged on her armchair, with Brody perched on her lap. The others piled onto the couch.

Noah and Vincent had stacked a sizeable pile of firewood beside the fireplace. After a brief break from chopping limbs off of a dead tree into firewood-sized pieces, they were exhausted, but Vincent insisted they needed to get to work making the aforementioned weapons. Apparently, his plan was to make homemade pepper spray and a flamethrower. It was ingenious, really, what Vincent had come up with so quickly, especially because it was all easily made with items she had around the cabin. Camille couldn't help but admire his intelligence.

Robert had always been crafty like that too. He was a skilled artisan and woodworker. He had even made the kitchen table in the cabin.

Leah stood from her position between Ava and Vincent on the couch and wandered around the room. She looked like she was snooping, stopping every so often to inspect something in the cabin. Camille watched her, eyes narrowed, and wondered what she was searching for.

Was Leah onto her? If she was, then Camille needed to do something about it. Either something to make Leah stop suspecting Camille, or something to make her so scared that she would stop. But which one should she choose? The first option didn't sound like much fun.

Leah glanced at the typewriter. Camille hastily stood, not wanting Leah to read anything she'd written. Her book was her secret project, one they couldn't know about. That would be a surprise for later. She wasn't ready for that revelation just yet.

"What's your book about, anyway?" Leah interrupted the uncomfortable, prolonged silence that had befallen them.

"It's about four people camping in the woods who are stuck in a cabin with a stranger and, for some unexplained reason, they can't return home," Camille said with a lighthearted chuckle.

Noah emitted a startled laugh at Camille's response, and a choking sound came from him afterward. He coughed and cleared his throat.

"Sorry, I was eating a brownie, and it went down the wrong pipe," Noah explained, brushing stray crumbs from his shirt.

"You don't have to apologize, Noah. Are you all right?" Camille asked, peering at him intently.

Noah coughed again, covering his mouth with his hand. "Yeah, I think so," he finally replied in a hoarse voice. He cleared his throat again.

Ava turned to her boyfriend and clapped her hand to her mouth when she saw him. Noah's face was becoming redder by the second. His eyes watered, and his nose scrunched up. He looked like he was holding back from coughing more, but suddenly, a coughing fit overtook him.

Ava clapped him on the back. "Are you okay?"

Noah shook his head, unable to speak. His cheeks were puffy and red, and sweat rolled down his face.

Vincent took charge of the situation. "Are you choking? Can you breathe?" he asked Noah. Before Noah could muster up a response, he turned to Camille. "Do you have a first aid kit?"

"Well, yes," she replied unsurely. "But I'm not sure what good that will do him. He's fine. It's just a little coughing. Perhaps from eating the brownies too quickly? He shoved them in his mouth so fast I don't see how he could have chewed them."

Noah continued coughing and gasped for air, his face turning from red to purple. He clutched at his throat, struggling to breathe and unable to form words. Ava stared at him helplessly, probably wondering what she could do to make him stop coughing.

"Someone call 911!" Ava yelled, her light brown eyes wildly looking around the cabin.

Camille sat at the edge of her armchair, holding Brody in her arms, watching the scenario play out. She stroked Brody's fur and kept the smile from spreading across her face. "You're welcome to use my phone if you're able to contact someone."

"He isn't allergic to anything, is he?" Leah asked Ava while Vincent ran into the kitchen.

After a few seconds, Camille heard Vincent slam the phone back down. He came back into the family room with a frustrated expression on his handsome face.

"What is it?" Camille asked.

"The phone call wouldn't go through." Vincent went over to Noah.

"Oh, that's a pity. It's difficult to make calls sometimes from all the way out here," Camille said.

Vincent shook his head. "Yeah, but the call to the towing company went through earlier. It doesn't make any sense. Why did the phone suddenly stop working?"

Ava was becoming inconsolable, with tears streaming down her face as her boyfriend continued to fight for breath. "What do we do? Help him!"

Vincent pulled Noah off the couch. Adjusting Noah's position on the floor, Vincent administered the Heimlich maneuver. After several attempts, nothing changed. Noah kept coughing. Another minute went by. Then, he passed out. Either from the exertion of coughing so hard or from the lack of oxygen.

"Oh my God! Noah!" Ava cried, rushing forward to her boyfriend. "Is he going to die? What's wrong with him?" She pulled his head into her lap and looked hopelessly at the others as tears continued to fall.

Tears covered Leah's face too, and she moved near Ava to comfort her. She wrapped her arm around her sister's shoulders.

Vincent checked Noah's pulse and grimaced. "It's faint, but he still has a pulse. I'm not sure what else to do. I only have basic first aid and CPR training. Does anyone else know anything that could help?" He questioned his friends, then turned to Camille.

Camille nodded and picked up Brody from her lap, placing him gently on the floor. "I can help. All you have to do is promise to stay in the cabin with me. Forever."

"Wh—what? We can't stay here forever! Our parents are probably worried out of their minds about us!" Ava said.

Camille shook her head slowly. "No, not you. Just Vincent." She turned her gaze back to Vincent. "What do you say, Vincent? Will you stay here with me to save your friend? Or will you let him die?"

Leah hugged Ava, holding her tightly and whispering reassurances. She appeared to be ignoring Camille's offer, which was probably for the best.

"Vincent? I'm going to need an answer," Camille snapped, annoyed that he was ignoring her and hadn't answered in the affirmative. All he needed to do was say yes, and this would all be over.

"This is insane! I'm not staying here with you. And how do you plan on saving him, anyway? Do you have some training or medical equipment stashed away that we don't know about? Because if you did, why didn't you say something sooner? What can you do to help him that none of us has tried?" Vincent said, a horrified expression passing over his face like a shadow.

Camille's face darkened. "I'm *not* insane," she said through gritted teeth. "You sound just like *him* now. He wanted me locked up when I wouldn't listen to him anymore. He was going to get rid of me. Is that what you're trying to do too?" Her eyes darted around the room in a paranoid manner. "Well, you can't! I'm the one in charge here." Her voice crackled with power.

"Please save him if you know how to," Ava said through her sobs. She swiped at her mascara-streaked cheeks. "Please don't let him die. I can't lose him."

Camille turned to Ava. "What will you give me if I save him?" she asked, her eyes glittering with interest.

"Wha—what do you me—mean?" Ava stuttered.

"If I save your boyfriend's life, what will you do for me in return?" Camille repeated.

"Anything! I—I'll d—do anything!" Ava cried, unable to stop more tears from cascading down her cheeks.

Camille nodded satisfactorily. "Good. That's what I wanted to hear." She moved closer to Noah. "I'm going to need you all to go wait in the spare bedroom while I do this, but I promise I'll save Noah."

"Why can't we stay in here? What are you going to do to him?" Vincent glared at Camille.

He didn't seem to trust her anymore. That was too bad.

"I'd rather not reveal my methods to four strangers," Camille replied tersely as she hovered over Noah's unconscious body. "Do you want him to die or not?"

"We'll leave! Just save him," Ava pleaded, stumbling to her feet and retreating to the spare bedroom, wiping her eyes as she left the room.

Leah chased her, then Vincent followed soon after, with a resigned sigh and one last helpless glance toward Noah.

Camille checked to make sure the door to the spare bedroom was closed and that they were all in there. Then she went to her desk and sat down in front of her typewriter. Brody trotted over and curled up near her feet, as usual.

Camille cracked her knuckles and lightly rested her fingers on top of the keys. As she typed, the keys glowed with power.

She typed,

While the others were in the spare bedroom, miraculously, Noah woke up with no further issues. He stopped coughing and could breathe again, no worse for the wear.

Camille went to get the other three to tell them to come back out to the main room.

"What happened?" Noah asked, appearing dazed when he woke up and saw everyone looking at him with various expressions of concern on their faces.

"You were coughing so hard you couldn't breathe. You fell unconscious and then..." Ava could barely speak through her stream of tears.

"What did you do? How did you save him?" Leah asked, with a mixture of wonder and fear in her voice.

A smile cracked Camille's impassive face. "That's for me to know and for you to find out when the time is right."

Camille was about to call to the others that they could leave the guest room, but as she headed down the hall, inspiration struck her yet again. Quickly, Camille sprinted back over to her typewriter. This time, she didn't bother to sit in her desk chair. Instead, she hunched over her desk, her fingers flying across the keys as she typed as fast as she could. As she typed, the typewriter glowed. She could almost feel the power coursing through her as she wrote the next scene.

When the scene was nearly complete, she paused her hasty typing for a few seconds to think. She didn't have enough time to write the next scene, so she would have to find time for that later, but this should do for now. She sat in her chair, finishing the last paragraph of the scene, then leaned back slightly to reread what she had written.

The front door wouldn't open. The doorknob wouldn't turn, no matter how hard Vincent and Noah tried to open the door or how much strength and force they exerted. But that wasn't the only terrifying thing that occurred in the moments after they decided they wanted to leave Camille's cabin for good.

While they had been preoccupied with the front door being stuck, all the windows in the house had vanished, as if by magic. Bewildered and now scared about what had happened, Vincent and the others futilely tried to find a window they may have overlooked or another way to leave the cabin. But it was to no avail. There was no way out.

Satisfied, she went to the spare bedroom to tell Vincent, Leah, and Ava they could come out now. The next phase in her plan was complete. She was ready for the real fun to begin.

Chapter 20: Leah

The three of them huddled together on the bed in the spare room. Leah did her best to comfort Ava, but the thought of losing Noah distressed her. Leah didn't know what Camille was doing out there. She hoped it worked. She couldn't bear to think about how Ava would cope with losing Noah. What if she relapsed and started drinking again? What if she couldn't stand to live without him and tried to hurt herself again?

"Do you think he's okay?" Ava peered up at her with bleary eyes, her mascara-streaked lashes covered in tears.

"I hope so," was all Leah could say as she held her sister, attempting to relieve her emotional pain in any way possible.

She turned to Vincent, who was blankly staring at the wall. Vincent hadn't said a word since they entered the bedroom. He hadn't believed her theory about Camille manipulating them and somehow trapping them in her cabin so they couldn't leave, or that she had sabotaged the van and the tow truck.

She couldn't worry about Vincent believing her right now, though. As long as Noah was in danger, that was her primary concern.

"We can't stay here." Vincent finally broke his silence.

"What?" Leah and Ava said simultaneously.

"We can't stay here," Vincent repeated. "It's not safe anymore. I don't know what Camille is doing out there, but I think she's involved in something... dark. I'm not saying she's a witch, but—"

"But it would make an awful lot of sense if she was," Leah finished for him, realizing where Vincent's mind was. She was relieved he finally understood what she had been trying to explain to him. If only he had believed her sooner, they might have been saved from some of their troubles.

Ava gasped and sat up straighter. "Do you really think she's—"

Before Ava could finish her sentence, the bedroom door was flung open to reveal a grinning Camille.

"You all can come out now," Camille said, gesturing expectantly for them to follow her.

Vincent left the room first, with Leah and Ava following closely behind him, holding hands. Ava's grip on Leah's hand tightened the closer they got to Noah.

Camille waved an arm toward Noah and said, "Ta-da!" as if she was a magician who had just pulled off a magic trick and not someone who had mysteriously brought a dying man back to life.

"What happened?" Noah asked, appearing dazed when he woke up.

Everyone looked at him with various expressions of concern on their faces.

"You were coughing so hard you couldn't breathe. You fell unconscious and then..." Ava could barely speak through her stream of tears.

"What did you do? How did you save him?" Leah asked, with a mixture of wonder and fear in her voice.

It had to be something like dark magic. What did Camille do? And what were they dealing with if they couldn't leave?

A smile cracked Camille's impassive face. "That's for me to know, and for you to find out... eventually."

Ava kneeled beside Noah, smoothing his spiky, blond hair down and telling him how much she loved him. Leah watched her sister and Noah, thankful he seemed to be okay. An eerie feeling had settled over her ever since Vincent had voiced what she had wondered too. But she had been too scared to say it out loud.

The words repeated in her head, 'I think she's involved in something... dark. I'm not saying she's a witch, but...'

The thought that Camille was a witch echoed through her mind. How could they find out the truth? And how could they ensure all four of them escaped the cabin alive?

Chapter 21: Camille

Camille's guests each checked on Noah to make sure he was okay. They surrounded him with comfort, love, and reassurances that everything would be fine. Noah seemed shaken, but he didn't remember what had happened. *Probably for the best*, Camille thought.

Ava sat on the rug in the middle of the room, cradling Noah's head on her lap. He was still lying on the floor, trying to get his bearings. He seemed confused about the situation, while Ava muttered to him over and over that he would be okay. Leah and Vincent stood protectively near them and kept darting looks at Camille as if she were a rabid dog bracing for an attack. What did they think was going to happen?

They couldn't have figured out her secret yet, but clearly, they knew something was off. Without learning more, they couldn't piece together the truth, though. They didn't know enough. Camille debated if she should let them sweat a little longer, or if she should give them a hint about what had really happened. Which plan would have more of an effect? And which choice would be more fun for her? Decisions, decisions...

Ava looked up at her from her position on the floor, bent over Noah. Tears had finally stopped falling from her eyes, and she appeared to be pulling herself together at last. Her eyes were red and bloodshot from crying; streaks of mascara marred her tanned cheeks. Seeing Noah almost die must have shaken her up. It was a fresh change to see the selfish girl show some emotion. Good. Now maybe they would all listen to her.

"How did you save him?" Ava asked in a soft voice, as if she was timid—the complete opposite of how she normally acted. She sniffled and wiped her nose with the back of her hand.

Camille shook her head firmly. "I already said I can't tell you that. Please don't ask me again, or you'll regret it."

Ava's eyes widened, and she nodded, diverting her gaze from Camille and back to Noah.

"Why?" Leah asked, turning to Camille with a fierce look in her eyes.

"Why what?" Camille tilted her head to the side.

"Why did you save him?" Leah asked.

Camille chuckled and stroked Brody's soft fur lovingly. "Why wouldn't I? I wasn't about to let someone die in my home. What would I have done with the body?"

Leah and Ava both gasped. It probably wasn't the answer they wanted to hear, but it was the truth.

"He doesn't have any allergies, and he's never had any major health issues. He rarely gets sick. I don't think he's even had a cold since I met him. So, I'm still confused about what happened. I need to know so it doesn't happen again. We're too far away from a hospital to get help if something else happens," Ava said, begging for answers.

"That's true. I think the nearest hospital is fifty miles away. You could never make it there in time if something else were to happen," Camille said, continuing to stroke Brody, who sighed happily at the extra attention. "Even if the phone call had gone through, I don't think an ambulance would have made it in time to save him."

"That doesn't answer my question," Ava said, her voice rising. "Noah had a violent coughing fit out of nowhere, fell unconscious, and you made us leave the room so you could save him... Do you... have medical training? What did you do to him?"

Noah's eyebrows scrunched together. He looked curiously at Camille, most likely wondering what had happened to him.

"I'm not sure what you're accusing me of, but I didn't do anything except save his life—something none of you were capable of. Noah would be dead right now if it wasn't for me, so you're welcome," Camille snapped, losing her cool.

The least the snotty teenagers could do was be grateful to her for what she did. She didn't *have* to save him, after all. She could have let him die. Then what would they be saying to her right now?

"As soon as Noah recovers, we're leaving," Vincent said.

Leah and Ava nodded rapidly, quick to agree with the so-called leader of their little group.

"We're going to need food and supplies to take with us to make it back to the van..." Vincent said, trailing off.

"How will we get there?" Ava sobbed.

"The van still needs a new battery! Even if we make it back, we can't drive home. If the engine won't start, we can't drive anywhere," Leah said as her face reddened.

"Shit. You're right," Vincent agreed. He ran his hands through his ponytail and sighed.

"*I won't tolerate any swearing in my house,*" Camille said with more than a hint of warning in her voice, snapping her head to look at Vincent so he knew she was serious.

The air in the cabin seemed to cool. Camille's frosty attitude was palpable. She hoped they knew the danger lurking in the cabin and that they realized the gravity of the situation.

"Sorry," Vincent said, tightening his jaw. He played with his ponytail again and squinted in concentration.

"What are we going to do, then? How will we get home?" Ava asked, clutching Noah.

"Okay," Vincent said. "We obviously don't have a vehicle, supplies, or a way to get home—"

"Thanks, Mr. Obvious. You're being really helpful." Ava rolled her eyes. She seemed to have recovered from her timid act she had been playing earlier.

"No one else is coming up with any solutions. What's your brilliant idea, then?" Vincent retorted, glaring at Ava.

"Hey, leave her alone." Noah pushed himself up onto his elbows and stood on trembling legs. He made his way to the couch and leaned back into the cushions with a heavy sigh.

Ava followed him and put her arm around him. Once Ava had settled next to her boyfriend, she said, "We need to call someone to help us. It's our only chance."

"Well, duh. But who are we going to call? Our families are all the way in Michigan. What are your parents going to do? Drive here to come pick us up?" Vincent said skeptically. "Besides, when I tried calling 911 earlier, the call didn't go through. Unless it started working again? I suppose it's worth a shot."

Camille moved to her armchair while they argued. She folded her hands in her lap, only for Brody to realize she had moved to the armchair and whine at her until she allowed him to jump up next to her. "When the snowstorm hit, I assumed the phone lines went down. It might work now."

"Hmm, strange. I didn't think about it until now, but the power didn't go out during the snowstorm," Vincent said, stroking his chin.

"It did during the night, for a bit," Camille hastily responded. "You were all asleep."

"But we were able to call for the tow truck, so I'm sure it's fine. I can call our parents. I'm sure they're the most likely to answer right away," Leah said, glancing at Ava, who nodded in agreement.

"Go ahead," Camille said.

"Great, thanks." Leah stood and went into the kitchen to make the call.

The rest of them waited in silence for Leah to return. A few minutes later, she came back into the room, her shoulders slumped.

"What is it?" Vincent rushed over to Leah and placed his hands on her shoulders.

"No one answered. In fact, the call didn't go through. Either the phone lines are down or something is wrong with the phone. There was only a dial tone."

Chapter 22: Leah

Vincent pulled her into an embrace. She hugged him back and leaned into his chest, thankful for his steady presence throughout this entire ordeal. He seemed to be the only calm, rational person here, besides her, of course. She wouldn't have gotten through this situation without him. *But we aren't out of it yet*, she reminded herself. They weren't safe until they were out of Camille's cabin and back at home.

"Noah, are you feeling better?" Vincent asked, abruptly ending the hug and going over to the couch to stand by Noah and Ava.

"I think so." Noah stood and stretched his arms out, then ambled around the room, testing his stamina. "Yeah, I feel fine now."

"Are you sure? You don't feel like you can't breathe, or like you're going to pass out again?" Vincent inquired, squinting at Noah.

Noah shook his head. "Nope."

"Good, then let's get out of here." Vincent went to the makeshift flame thrower and pepper spray weapons they had created earlier, then gestured for Leah and the others to come with him.

"Camille, I wish I could say it's been great, but... well, it's been a strange three days," Vincent said.

Vincent undid the deadbolt across the front door, then put his hand on the doorknob and attempted to turn it. The doorknob stayed firmly in place, unmoving. He stared at it for a few seconds, then tried twisting the doorknob the other way.

"Is it stuck or something?" Vincent stepped back slightly, examining the door with a hand on his chin. "Is there a trick to opening it?" He tried yanking on the doorknob again, this time with both hands, but it refused to turn.

"No tricks here," Camille said. She swung her arms as she came over to them.

"Nah, you just gotta give it some muscle, man," Noah said, putting on a show of pumping up his arms and showing off his huge biceps, then joining Vincent by the front door. "You really need to join me at the gym some time."

"You're still recovering. Are you sure you should—" Vincent started, but Noah waved him off.

Noah gave a dramatic flourish, grabbed the doorknob, and attempted to turn it both ways as well, but the doorknob still didn't move. He tried turning it each way again. The door remained locked.

As the seconds ticked by, Leah became more worried and assumed her twin felt the same. If they couldn't leave through the front door, then how could they get out of the cabin?

"What the hell?" Noah mumbled, grabbing the doorknob and exerting more pressure on it futilely. "It's like it's broken. It's not turning at all." He stared at Vincent, his pale blond eyebrows scrunched together.

"What do we do?" Vincent replied.

Noah responded by slamming his shoulder into the door several times, hoping to break it down.

Vincent stepped away from the door and began circling the room. "Stop, Noah. It's not working. Maybe we can smash out a window?"

"That won't be happening in my home. You can't destroy my property!" Camille protested. She clenched her hands by her sides; her fiery red hair framed her face.

"We can, and we will. We're leaving, no matter what we have to do," Vincent said.

Vincent went to the side of the cabin where they all had noticed a window before, across from Camille's desk and typewriter. For a few seconds, he blankly stared at the empty wall, then looked back at them with an expression of complete terror.

As soon as Leah's gaze landed on the spot where the window should have been, she realized what was wrong. The rustic wall was free of any decorations—completely empty, in fact. The window was gone.

Chapter 23: Camille

Oh, this is too much fun, Camille thought gleefully. She should have done this ages ago. The first time hadn't given her so much satisfaction, but this was different. The characters truly made all the difference, and this time was better than ever. Pride shimmered throughout her mind for making it happen. They were stuck here because of her. She was a genius.

They couldn't leave through the front door because the doorknob wouldn't turn. They had realized the window by her desk was gone. What would they try next? The other windows? How else could they exit her home? There was no way out. She had thought of everything.

As if on cue, Vincent and Noah split up and walked around the cabin, searching for the other windows that used to be there.

"Look for any viable entry point to escape from," Vincent told Noah. "Even if it seems like a tight fit, we'll make it work. Leah and Ava are small. We can send them out first if we can't get out. Then they can go get help for us."

Leah and Ava huddled by the front door, with their arms wrapped around each other. Neither of them had moved since the revelation that the window was gone.

"What happened to the window?" Leah asked, her face drawn and pale. "A window can't just disappear!"

Ava shook her head, her nails digging into Leah's skin. "I don't know. Vince and Noah will figure something out. There has to be a way out."

Several minutes later, Vincent and Noah returned. Noah nodded at something Vincent had said while they were searching the bedrooms.

"Okay, so all the other windows are gone too," Vincent began.

"How?" Leah moved toward Vincent and dropped Ava's hands from hers. "How did they disappear?"

"Leah, I know this is insane and impossible, but all I care about right now is getting the four of us out of here and safely home. We don't have time to analyze the logic of it. If we do, we'll be here forever trying to figure it out," Vincent said. "We might never understand what happened, but I promise I'll get you home."

"Okay," Leah said softly, clearly not wanting to drop the subject, but doing so anyway.

"Like I was saying, all the windows are gone," Vincent continued.

"Then how do we leave?" Ava asked, her eyes shooting haphazardly around the room as she looked for an escape route. Maybe she hoped she would spot something that Vincent and Noah had missed.

Camille almost laughed. There was no way out. She had made sure of that. *Oh, what fun this is!*

"The only way to leave is through the fireplace." Vincent pointed to the brick fireplace on the far back wall of the main room.

"What?" Camille said, suddenly fearful.

The fireplace? She had made sure they couldn't turn the doorknob, and all the windows were gone, but what about the fireplace? Why hadn't she considered that as an exit? Of course, they would be resourceful if they were desperate. How had she missed that?

"The fireplace," Vincent said again impatiently as he moved in front of the brick-lined fireplace, "is the only way to leave."

Over the course of the day, the fire had dwindled and gone out. Only small wisps of smoke rose from the logs as evening struck. Leah followed Vincent over to the fireplace and bent down onto her knees so she could tilt her head and look up the chimney. Camille wasn't sure what she was searching for, but it didn't seem good.

"What will we do? Climb up the chimney? I'm afraid of heights," Leah said in a shrill voice. She groped for Vincent's hand to steady her as she rose to her feet.

"I'll go first to make sure it's safe," Vincent reassured her. He brought her hand to his lips and kissed it.

"What? No, Vince! I don't want you to risk your life. What if you fall?" Leah pleaded with her boyfriend.

"That's clever, I'll give you that," Camille said, moving near the fireplace. She placed her hands on her hips. "But how will you climb the walls? And even if you make it to the top and manage to climb out of the chimney, what will you do once you're on the roof of the cabin? It's too high to jump."

"She's right," Noah said with a resigned sigh, rubbing his forehead as if to get rid of a headache. "I don't think we would survive a fall from that high. Or we would be seriously injured, at the very least. And we still don't have transportation or a way to get home, even if we get out of here."

"If we had my camping supplies, we could make it work. I have a twenty-foot-long rope in the van," Vincent said.

"Well, the van is on the side of the road miles away," Ava replied in a snarky tone. "And we don't have any rope here, so what are we going to do?"

"Hold on, let me think." Vincent leaned against the brick wall and tapped it anxiously.

Leah put her arm in Vincent's and clung onto him, like she was clinging onto a life raft to avoid drowning in the middle of the ocean. Silence ensued while they all thought through the possibilities.

"This is ridiculous," Camille shattered the sudden silence and sneered at them. "No one will be leaving. As Noah so helpfully pointed out, you wouldn't survive the fall from the roof, so there's no point in trying to climb the inside of the chimney." Camille appraised the chimney with an eyebrow raised. "I don't remember the last time I cleaned the chimney, anyway. Who knows what's living in there?"

Ava shuddered, and Noah kissed her cheek. "We'll find another exit," Noah promised her.

Vincent nodded. "We will, I swear. I'll get you guys out of here if it's the last thing I do."

"Don't make promises you can't keep, Vincent," Camille snarled.

Chapter 24: Leah

More than anything, Leah wanted for her boyfriend's promise to be true, but she was losing hope. They had been through so much together over the past three days. She didn't see how they would make it home, but she still believed in Vincent. They were in an impossible situation, but Vincent would save them. He always did, and that was one thing she loved about him.

Vincent always came through for her, often sacrificing his own well-being. She was all he had left, so she knew he would do anything to make sure she was okay. And he would save Ava and Noah too, because they were important to her.

Leah scoured the main room of the cabin again, futilely searching for a hidden compartment or a secret trap door they hadn't known about, wondering if there was another exit they had overlooked. But of course, there wasn't. This wasn't some fantasy movie taking place in a magical cabin. It was a very real secluded cabin in the middle of the woods. If anything, it was more like a horror movie where the main characters stood no chance of survival against the evil witch.

Leah shook her head, making her coarse, brown hair, now greasy from being unwashed, fling around her shoulders. She didn't want to believe

Camille was evil, but she couldn't ignore everything that had happened the last three days. The thought of being trapped in a cabin with a witch was terrifying. Besides, Camille had saved Noah's life. Would an evil witch save someone in danger? Maybe so, but why did she save him?

Whatever Camille was, she had made it clear she didn't want them to leave. But what did she want from them? They had been strangers until three days ago, so what was her obsession with making them stay in her cabin with her forever? Was she just lonely, or was she unhinged? And how had she saved Noah when nothing they tried had worked?

Dozens of questions threatened to overwhelm Leah, and she gasped for breath as she tried to slow down her racing mind.

"Hey, are you okay, sweetie?" Vincent asked, securely wrapping an arm around her waist to steady her shaking body.

Leah nodded numbly, her mind still tumbling with questions about Camille.

Vincent stared at her with his kind brown eyes. "Are you sure?"

"Yeah," Leah said, realizing Vincent must have had a flashback to when Noah had stopped being able to breathe and fell unconscious. She took a deep breath and exhaled. "I'm fine."

Ava's and Noah's faces showed identical expressions of concern.

Leah mustered a smile, and Vincent led her over to the couch. "Here, sit down for a minute. I'll get you some water."

Vincent vanished into the kitchen, with Camille trailing after him. Leah narrowed her eyes as she watched Camille and Vincent go into the kitchen together. It's not like she didn't trust him, but—

Ava placed a gentle hand on her shoulder. "Calm down. You know he won't do anything. Vincent made it perfectly clear how he feels about Camille. He won't cheat on you with her."

Leah huffed, but she knew her sister was right. Probably.

A minute later, but after what seemed like an eternity to Leah, Vincent returned to her side with a glass of water and handed it to her with a dramatic bow. Leah giggled and thanked him.

"You're sweet, but so weird sometimes," she told him with a grin. She knew he was trying to lighten the mood and make her smile.

Vincent grinned back. "But that's what you like about me, right?"

Leah merely shook her head and drank the entire glass of water in only a few gulps. She had most likely been dehydrated. She hadn't focused on meeting her daily water consumption while their lives had been at risk. Technically, their lives were *still* at risk. After she finished, she set the glass on the coffee table, making sure it was on one of the kitschy-looking crocheted coasters. She figured Camille would jump at any opportunity to chew her out if she didn't use it.

When Leah's gaze drifted away from the coffee table, she realized Camille hadn't returned from the kitchen. "Where is she?" she whispered to Vincent.

"Still in the kitchen, I guess," he said with a shrug, trying too hard to appear nonchalant.

"Why did she follow you in there?" Leah asked.

"To show me where the glasses were," Vincent said.

"That's dumb. You could have found them on your own."

"I know. That's what I told her."

Leah rolled her eyes. Was Camille looking for excuses to be alone with Vincent? Why was she so intent on flirting with him when she knew he was dating Leah? Plus, Camille was supposedly married, and she had to be at least ten years older than Vincent. That was creepy, not to mention gross.

Just then, Camille came out of the kitchen and strode right over to the stack of board games they had left underneath the coffee table after the game night, which seemed like an eternity ago. She picked up the stack of games and set them on the coffee table. There weren't any windows to see out of, or any way to determine what color the sky was outside or if the sun had set yet, but Leah assumed it had to be well into the evening by now.

"Who fancies a board game?" Camille waved around Trivial Pursuit with obvious excitement, any trace of anger from earlier now gone.

The teenagers stared at Camille, wondering what the hell she was thinking.

Noah spoke up first. "What makes you think we want to play a board game with you?" He snorted.

Camille's smile froze in place, and her lower lip jutted out like a stubborn child whose mother just told them no ice cream before dinner. "No one wants to play a game with me?"

At that moment, Brody yelped as if he agreed with Camille.

No one answered Camille. Then Leah made a decision. A decision she hoped would save their lives.

Chapter 25: Camille

Leah smiled sweetly at her before saying, "Of course we'll play games with you, Camille. We all love playing board games. Right?" Leah made eye contact with her friends, and they all nodded in agreement.

Vincent piped up next. "Sure, we will."

Camille clapped her hands together excitedly. "Oh, I love nights like this, playing board games, surrounded by friends."

Noah raised an eyebrow, which he might have thought Camille would miss, but she noticed everything. They had no clue how closely she watched their every move.

"Which one shall we play first?" Camille asked them, spreading out the stack of games so everyone could see the names.

"We'll decide. How about you go get us some snacks? We haven't eaten much today, and we need to keep up our strength," Vincent suggested with his charming smile on display.

Camille melted under his gaze. She couldn't resist that smile. "I would be happy to. Do you mind helping me? It will be a lot for me to carry all by myself," she said, batting her eyelashes at him.

Leah's fierce expression implied she wanted to slice Camille apart, piece by piece, and Camille snickered as Vincent agreed to help her.

When Camille was in the kitchen, she turned to Vincent. "Do you mind opening up that cupboard and grabbing something for me from the top shelf?" She pointed to the cupboard in front of her. "I can't reach it, and you're so tall."

"Sure." Vincent opened the cupboard, then scanned the top shelf. "What were you trying to reach?"

Camille pressed herself against Vincent's back, wrapping her arms around his waist. Just as she settled her head onto his shoulder and her lips puckered to kiss the back of his neck, he flung her off of him and spun around wildly to face her.

"What. Are. You. Doing?" he asked, with his teeth clenched and breathing rapidly.

A smile crept over Camille's face. "I was just giving you a hug, Vincent. No need to get into a tizzy, dear."

Vincent unclenched his jaw and his shoulders lowered slightly, as if he was attempting to relax. "Why?"

Camille tilted her head to the side. "Well, friends can hug, can't they?"

"Uh, I guess..." was Vincent's unsure answer as he scratched the back of his head. "What did you want from this cupboard?" He changed the subject clumsily.

"Oh, nothing. All the snacks are in there." Camille pointed to the cupboard to the right of the one Vincent had opened. She took too much glee in the explosion of anger and confusion displayed across his handsome face.

"But, then why did you—" he protested.

"Vince." She moved closer to him, placing her arms on the kitchen counter so their bodies were pressed together.

Vincent tried to lean back, but he was against the counter and had nowhere to go. "What are you doing, Camille? I'm with Leah."

"Stop fighting this. I know you feel it too. The passion and lust between us. There's no point in continuing this charade. I promise I won't tell Leah," Camille said, placing her hand on Vincent's cheek.

Vincent didn't move for several seconds, long enough that Camille wondered if she had seduced him and he would really give in. She leaned in, preparing herself for the ecstasy of kissing this wonderful man who reminded her so much of Robert, but he shoved her hand off of his cheek. He rummaged in the cupboard, grabbed an armful of snacks, and retreated to the main room without another word to her.

Camille stayed rooted in place for a moment, wondering what she had done wrong. It was supposed to work, wasn't it? She was the one in control. She had all the power. He shouldn't have been able to say no. He was supposed to be compelled to follow her wishes. So why hadn't Vincent succumbed to her?

Should she have tried Noah instead? His will was weaker, but no—he wasn't the one she wanted. Vincent was the reincarnation of her husband, her Robert, and thus, he was the man she wanted to be with.

After another moment of pondering the situation, Camille grabbed a few more snacks, plastered a fake smile onto her face, and went back into the main room to join the others.

They all watched her as she entered, implying they had been talking about her before she reentered the room. She didn't want to reveal that she knew, so she acted like everything was fine. Brody was curled up in her armchair. She nudged him gently. He opened his eyes and growled, probably annoyed that she had woken him and moved him over to sit down. He quickly fell back asleep after he settled in her lap.

"What game did we decide on, then?" Camille asked, attempting to sound chipper. If she acted like nothing was wrong, maybe they would want to stay. She needed to make sure they didn't leave. She couldn't bear to think about what would happen if they did. Besides, the game wasn't over yet.

"It doesn't matter—" Ava said.

At the same time, Vincent said, "Mouse Trap."

They both burst out laughing.

"Whatever is fine," Leah said, shrugging her shoulders.

Camille picked up Mouse Trap, deciding she would go with Vincent's choice. "Okay, then. Let's play this one." She turned to Ava, smiling slightly. "Do you mind if I bring out some wine? I know you're sober, but—"

Ava shrugged. "It's fine. I won't be tempted or whatever. It's been over six months since I last had a drink."

Noah patted Ava's arm, then pulled her closer to him. "You sure, babe?"

Ava nodded, nestling into Noah's shoulder for a moment. "I'll be fine. I'm not that weak," she said with a smirk, tossing her golden hair over her shoulder.

Ava's hair somehow still looked glossy and healthy, even after days of camping, hiking, and trauma. Some women were just lucky, Camille supposed. She had never been one of those women, and she envied them. The type of women husbands cheated on their wives for. The type of woman she needed to be to tempt Vincent. But she couldn't think about that. It hadn't worked. She needed a new plan.

Camille went into the kitchen to find a nice bottle of wine and four wine glasses. She assumed everyone except Ava would want to drink. When she carried everything back into the main room, Ava eyed the wine bottle with an intense longing in her eyes. Camille poured the wine into the glasses and proposed a toast.

"A toast to what?" Ava asked, clutching a glass of water.

"A toast to new friends and new beginnings!" Camille exclaimed.

Everyone raised their glasses and repeated the toast in forced cheerful tones, sounding monotone. The glasses clinked together, eliciting euphoria throughout Camille as she waited for what was yet to come.

Chapter 26: Leah

After Camille took a sip from her glass of wine, Leah decided it was safe to drink. She greedily gulped down half of the glass. Wiping her mouth with the back of her hand, she sighed. She already felt a buzz.

Leah didn't drink much anymore because of Ava, so it felt nice to enjoy a drink and relax. If they were stuck in this godforsaken cabin, then she might as well drink some wine and make the best of the situation. If she was drunk, maybe she would feel better equipped to deal with the craziness.

The others soon followed suit. After they finished the bottle Camille had brought out, she retreated to the kitchen and brought out more wine. Apparently, Camille was a heavy wine drinker, and she had an entire collection of wine in the kitchen. Leah rarely drank wine—she was only seventeen and preferred wine coolers—but she didn't care about the bitter taste right now.

By the time they had finished two bottles of wine, they were all having fun playing board games, laughing, and joking around with each other.

Leah noticed Ava had been unusually quiet, so she nudged her sister with her shoulder.

"You doing all right?" Leah asked, trying not to slur her words. A lightheaded feeling had drifted over her.

"Fine," Ava said, before making her next move in the game.

"Are you having *fuuun*, babe?" Noah asked, grabbing Ava's shoulders and lightly shaking her.

Ava smiled with her lips tightly pressed together. "Yup."

Vincent burst out laughing at something Camille had said to him, and he laughed so hard that he slapped his knee.

"What's so funny?" Leah asked as she turned her attention to Vincent and Camille.

"Oh, nothing. It was stupid," Vincent said with a grin, shaking his head.

Camille grinned back at Vincent. They were wrapped up in their own little world, and Leah didn't like that.

She scooted over until she was sitting on Vincent's lap, then wrapped her arms around his neck, straddling him, their faces inches apart. Leah leaned in and planted a kiss on her boyfriend's lips, then tangled her hands in his hair.

At first, he seemed to protest, but then he leaned into her body and returned the kiss eagerly until Ava pushed them apart, making Leah tumble backward off of the couch and onto the floor. Leah's head narrowly missed hitting the coffee table, and she gasped as she hit the floor. She rubbed her elbow where it struck the side of the table as she fell.

"Geez, what was that for?" Vincent glared at Ava, then stood and held out a hand to help Leah up.

Leah gratefully accepted his offer and let Vincent tuck her into his arms, so she was safe. She whimpered and rubbed her elbow again.

"You were making a fool of yourself," Ava said, rolling her eyes pointedly at Leah.

"Was I? I guess you would know," Leah retorted hotly, aggravated at her sister for her remark and for injuring her. Her cheeks warmed from the panic of almost hitting her head and the embarrassment of her sister calling her out.

"What's that supposed to mean?" Ava crossed her arms over her chest and stared her down.

"You know exactly what I meant. You did way worse things when you were drunk all the time. Noah doesn't even know the half of it. Like the back-to-school party you went to," Leah said, wanting to hurt her sister as much as she could in that moment.

"Stop it!" Ava said.

Leah continued on, not heeding her sister's plea, "And when you played strip poker with those guys, even though you were dating Noah." Leah felt giddy for about half a second before guilt slammed into her like a semi-truck.

The hurt was clear on Ava's face. "You promised you wouldn't tell anyone." She scrunched up her face, like she had when she was a kid, trying not to cry.

Leah wondered if she had taken it too far.

"Sorry," Leah offered halfheartedly, rubbing her elbow. "I shouldn't have said that."

"Sorry too," Ava said as tears rolled down her pink cheeks. "I wasn't trying to hurt you."

Camille interjected, "I need to get some writing done tonight. Do you all mind sleeping in the spare bedroom and my bedroom instead of out here? I can sleep on the couch again."

Leah glanced at Vincent, who nodded.

"Okay," Leah said. "I hope you're able to catch up on your writing."

Camille smiled; it stretched tightly across her face as if it was forced.

After drinking all that wine, Leah suddenly had to pee. Plus, she needed an excuse to leave the room after the awkward fight with her sister. She stood to use the bathroom, swaying on her feet as she moved down the hallway.

"Sweetie, are you all right? What are you doing?" Vincent held out an arm to steady her.

"Just going to the bathroom," she answered, trying her best to appear sober.

The room seemed to tilt sideways, and she barely made it to the bathroom. She nearly bumped into the wall as she turned the corner.

By the time Leah had washed her hands, nausea had bubbled up in her stomach. She was already in the bathroom, so she lifted the toilet seat and leaned over, instantly dry heaving into the toilet.

A few minutes later, a knock came from the bathroom door.

"Yeah?" Leah called out weakly, her hands shaking as she wiped her mouth with a piece of tissue.

"Are you okay? You've been in there for a while," Vincent said from outside the bathroom.

Leah heard him try to turn the doorknob, but she had locked the door.

"Mmhmm, be out in a minute."

Underneath the sink, Leah found mouthwash, rinsed out her mouth, and attempted to tame her frizzy, brown hair. She was a mess, but she wanted to keep up appearances. She didn't want Vincent to have any reason to check out other women. If her appearance wasn't perfect, he would be more likely to find someone else. Maybe even someone in the cabin. Someone who was interested in him. Like Camille.

She opened the door to find Vincent leaning against the wall in the hallway, waiting for her. He stepped forward and clasped her hands in his.

"Are you okay?" He frowned and rubbed her hands.

She nodded and squeezed his hands in reassurance. "Just feeling sick. I might have drunk too much."

Vincent chuckled. "Sorry. I'll get you some water, then we can go to bed if you want?"

"Sure."

Leah went back into the main room of the cabin to let everyone know. "I'm not feeling great, so Vincent and I are going to sleep. Night, everyone."

"Aww, you guys are lame!" Noah slapped the arm of the couch.

"We should all try to get some rest," she told them. "Tomorrow, we'll talk about our plans."

"Okay. Night, Leah," Ava said softly.

Leah waved goodbye and went into the master bedroom. She found a pair of pajamas in Camille's dresser and brushed her teeth, then slid under the covers, waiting for Vincent to return with some water. When he entered the bedroom, he handed her a glass and a plate of plain crackers.

"I thought this might help your stomach." Vincent settled in the bed next to her.

"Thanks. You're so sweet." Leah accepted the crackers and nibbled on them slowly, hoping her queasy stomach would settle. She had thrown up everything she ate earlier, so her stomach was empty. She drank the water and lay back down in bed.

"Do you think we'll find a way out?" she whispered, turning over to face Vincent. The thought of never escaping had entered her mind again. She couldn't help but wonder what they would do. How would they leave?

"Yes. I promise we'll get out of here," Vincent whispered back fiercely, his brown eyes shining. He stroked her hair. "I won't let anything happen to you. We're going to make it home safely. Okay?"

Leah nodded as sleep overtook her. She closed her eyes and felt Vincent press his lips to her forehead and mutter, "Goodnight, Leah," before she drifted off into a restless sleep.

Chapter 27: Camille

When her guests were in bed, Camille picked up Brody and carried his small, sleeping body over to her desk. She placed her beloved dog underneath her desk, so he could get comfortable in his plush dog bed. She tucked him into a small, fuzzy blanket, cocooning him in warmth, and sat down in her chair.

Now, what should she write next? Her guests were back in her cabin, with all the exits blocked or gone. That was the important thing. But what else could she do to deter them from getting home?

If they became adventurous and desperate, they could still try to leave through the chimney. Camille stared at her typewriter for a moment before typing the next chapter.

As her fingers pressed down on the keys, the typewriter glowed with a golden light, illuminating the almost completely darkened room. The more Camille wrote, the more inspired she became. The desire to continue writing fulfilled her. Before she knew it, she had almost finished the rest of her novel.

It would be simple enough to finish the last few chapters when she had some free time the next day. She just needed to make sure she had a bit of time for herself tomorrow.

Her eyes were growing heavy when Brody's snoring made her jump out of her chair. She was drifting off at her desk. She had been writing for hours. Camille checked the clock and realized with a jolt that it was just after 2 a.m. Time for sleep.

Camille picked Brody up and snuggled with him on the couch, pulling a heavy quilt over them and settling into a fitful sleep. She dreamed about four strangers trapped in a cabin in the woods with a writer.

Writers are powerful, she thought as she fell asleep. Writers had the power to create and destroy characters and even entire worlds. That kind of power was dangerous in the hands of the wrong person.

***

The next morning, the coffee maker bubbled away and the smell of freshly brewed coffee permeated the air. There was nothing quite like waking up to the aromatic scent of coffee and the anticipation of the first sip of the day.

She stretched her legs out over the arm of the couch and saw Brody's head peek out from underneath the quilt. Camille slid off of the couch and headed toward the kitchen, immediately smiling when she spotted a man with a tidy, long, brown ponytail bent over the coffee maker.

"Good morning, Vincent," Camille said cheerily, approaching him from behind.

He jumped and nearly dropped the glass coffeepot. Camille jerked out an arm to grab it, but he managed not to lose his grip. Her fingers grazed his as she let go.

"Oh, uh... Hi, Camille. You scared me." Vincent attempted to recover from his shock.

"I apologize. I woke up when I smelled the coffee brewing."

"Oh, sorry. I tried to be quiet. I'm an early riser, and I've been awake long enough that I couldn't lie in bed any longer. I needed some caffeine." Vincent reached into the cupboard to find a second mug for Camille. He poured the coffee into the mugs and handed one to her.

"Thank you." Camille grabbed the mug and took a seat at the kitchen table, expecting Vincent to join her. She stared at him expectantly, beckoning him to the table.

Vincent stood in front of the coffee maker for another few seconds, and she wondered what was going through his mind. Her eyes narrowed. If he didn't want to be here anymore, she could take care of that. He didn't know whom he was dealing with or that his life wasn't guaranteed. Everything was still up in the air, unless Camille changed her mind. His next decision could be his last one if he chose incorrectly.

Eventually, he pulled out the other chair and sat down across from her.

"No one else is awake yet, then?" Camille blew on her coffee to cool it off before taking the first sip. She did her best to calm her racing heart. Seconds before, she had contemplated murdering him, but she didn't want him to know that.

"Nope, they're all still asleep. Leah wasn't feeling great, so I wanted to let her rest," Vincent said, drinking his still steaming coffee right away as if the heat didn't bother him. He must have burned his mouth, though—it was piping hot.

"What's the plan for today?" Camille peered at him with her coffee mug still raised in front of her face, partially blocking her expression.

"Plan?" Vincent repeated dumbly, as if he didn't know what she was talking about.

But she knew better than that. He may try to play stupid, but Vincent was intelligent. Of course, he had a plan. For all she knew, he could have talked to the others while she was writing or when she was sleeping.

Camille set her coffee mug on the scratched wooden table and gestured with her hand impatiently. "Your escape plan. What is it? I'm curious." She leaned her elbows on the table and rested her chin on her hands, appraising him while she waited for his answer.

Vincent stared back at her, pausing with his mug partway to his mouth. He set it back down without taking a sip and shrugged. "There isn't one. We already tried all the exits and entry points. Getting out through the chimney was our last-ditch effort to leave, but that wasn't possible because we don't have rope or a safe way to get off the roof once we're outside. And even if we got out, we would still have to walk miles to find someone to help us. Or find a working phone to use. None of those options are great."

Camille dropped her chin from her hands and sat up straighter. "What if I promised to help you?"

Vincent appeared to study her, perhaps wondering if he should believe her after everything she had done to them. He pursed his lips. "Why would you do that? I thought you didn't want us to leave. You asked me to stay here with you forever."

"Vincent, you don't understand yet, do you? I'm only—"

"No, I don't understand any of this!" Vincent exploded, slamming his fist down on the rickety table. His coffee sloshed out of the mug. Camille resisted the urge to wipe up the spilled coffee immediately. "That's why we're stuck here. I don't know what powers you have or—"

Camille cut him off. "You know about my powers?" Her heart thudded erratically in her chest at Vincent's revelation. She wasn't sure if she was more terrified or thrilled about him finding out. What would happen when he knew the truth?

Vincent shook his head and backtracked. "I mean, just that you somehow made sure the door stayed locked, and you got rid of the windows. Plus, you saved Noah when it seemed like he was going to die. I don't know how you did it because nothing I tried was helping him. You aren't a trained nurse or something, are you? You're just a writer. It's not possible to be a… That's what I can't figure out. Are you…" He stopped talking, probably too scared to voice what he thought. He bit his lip and stared at his half-full coffee mug.

Maybe he thought if he didn't say it out loud, then it couldn't be true.

But the main thing was, he didn't know where her power came from. He had no clue what she could do to him and his friends. How much she could torture them until she finally let them go.

Well, she hadn't decided about that last part yet. Maybe she wouldn't ever let them leave. For the first time in ages, she was enjoying herself. Besides, she was the one in control for once. She should take advantage of her power as long as it was hers. She didn't know how long it would last, and she was still learning what worked and what didn't. Camille needed more time to test the limits of her power. She couldn't let them go yet.

Chapter 28: Leah

Leah couldn't remember the last time she had a hangover this bad. Probably when Ava had been in the worst of her drinking sprees, back when they went to random parties every weekend.

Leah could never keep up with Ava, though. Mostly, she accompanied Ava to keep an eye on her and make sure she didn't get into any real trouble—and she hadn't, mostly. There was only the one incident that had been truly awful, the thing that made Ava finally give up drinking. The thing Leah had so unabashedly reminded her of last night. But Leah didn't want to think about that, especially first thing in the morning when she had more pressing matters to worry about.

She sat up in bed and leaned against the headboard, trying to get her bearings and remember what had happened last night. Her head pounded as she thought about drinking all that wine and getting sick afterward. Vincent had been so sweet, checking on her and bringing her water and crackers. He always took care of her and looked out for her wellbeing. Vincent was the only guy she had ever dated who cared about her more than he cared about himself. He always put her first.

She stumbled out of bed and into the bathroom, putting on her clothes from the day before and readying herself for the day. She wasn't sure what today would bring, but she was trying to embody Vincent's persona and be prepared for anything. Who knew what crazy thing would happen today while they were stuck in this cabin? Leah couldn't guess what Camille had up her sleeves.

With her hair in two neat braids and her face washed, she went out into the main room of the cabin. No one was there other than Brody, who was lying in front of the fireplace, soaking in the fire's warmth. When Leah stood by him, his tail started wagging, thumping against the floorboards. She bent down to scratch between his ears, and his tail wagged even harder. Leah giggled and patted him on the head before sitting down next to him in front of the fire. She assumed Vincent was in the kitchen making coffee and waited for him to come out and join her.

A few minutes later, Camille and Vincent entered the room together. Leah pretended not to be bothered that they had been in the kitchen together while she was asleep, for God only knew how long. Instead, she smiled at them and waved hello.

"Good morning," she greeted them.

Vincent bent down to kiss the top of her head and said he would get her some coffee. Camille settled into her armchair, and Brody abandoned Leah for his owner's lap.

"How did you sleep?" Camille asked, holding a mug of coffee in her hands. The steam curled up toward her face.

"Pretty good, actually. Your bed is comfortable."

"Good. The couch, I'm afraid, is not the most comfortable," Camille said with a sarcastic chuckle.

"Oh, sorry about you giving up your bed again," Leah said awkwardly. She wasn't really sorry this time because now she knew all sorts of things about Camille, although she was certain they hadn't even begun to uncover the truth about their mysterious hostess.

"I do like the company, though. Sometimes I'm alone for so long that I forget what it's like to be around people. It's good for me to get some human interaction once in a while. Usually, I go into town about once a week—"

"Where's the closest town?" Leah asked, attempting to appear nonchalant despite her heart hammering away in her chest.

If a town was close enough, maybe they could reach it if they escaped. Then they could find a working phone and ask someone to help them get home. Or even find a police station and get help from local law enforcement.

"About twenty miles north of here. It's a small town, but there's a grocery store, a gas station, and a few other small shops. It's sufficient for replenishing my supplies when I'm running low. I like to stay stocked up because you never know what's going to happen out here, living in the mountains, away from civilization and technology," Camille said in a sinister tone. Or was Leah imagining it?

"I love small towns," Leah continued the conversation as if she was unbothered. "They're usually full of kind people, and they're so... unpretentious. Small business owners are more grateful to customers for their business because it's their livelihood, don't you think so?"

Camille blinked several times before she responded, "I suppose. I try to support small businesses when I can. Few large companies think having a location in the middle of nowhere is worth it."

"It would be nice to explore some other towns in the area. We only saw the rural part of Asheville while we were camping, and of course, we haven't seen much at all in the last few days."

Camille smiled broadly; the effort stretched her face in a cartoonish manner. "That's too bad. You're missing out on a lot of gorgeous scenery, local restaurants, and trendy shops. If you're ever back in the area—"

"*Back* in the area?" Leah let out a barking laugh. "You mean, if you ever let us leave. If we get away, we aren't coming back here."

Vincent returned, handed Leah a coffee mug, and settled next to her on the floor in front of the blazing fire. He leaned against her shoulder and settled comfortably beside her.

"Thanks," she said, after accepting the mug and staring into the fireplace.

Vincent must have heard the end of their conversation, but he didn't comment on the topic. Instead, he seemed determined to act as if everything was perfectly normal, which was unnerving to Leah, who felt trapped and suffocated in the confines of the small cabin. Especially with Camille sitting several feet away from them, plotting their demise. Vincent wrapped his arm around her shoulders and pulled her closer to him. Leah set her mug on the floor so she wouldn't spill her coffee. She rested her head on Vincent's shoulder and sighed in contentment.

At least I have Vincent, she thought for the hundredth time that week. He had done nothing wrong, so she needed to cool it and stop acting as if he was cheating on her with Camille. Or as if he was about to leave her. Vincent wouldn't do that to her. He had never showed signs of wandering eyes or being discontented with their relationship. The stress of the past four days was getting to her in the worst way and making her imagine things.

"Are the other two still sleeping?" Camille asked, her voice as sweet as iced tea.

Leah shrugged. "I guess so."

"It looks like it's just the three of us, then!" Camille wrapped a blanket around herself and tucked it around Brody too. "Does it feel chilly in here today?"

Leah moved away from Vincent and involuntarily leaned in closer to the fire, holding her hands out in front of herself to warm them. "Yeah, it does. Is the heat working?"

Vincent backed away from Leah and stood, his eyes drifting around the cabin. "Where's the thermostat? I can check it out and see what's going on."

"Oh no, that's fine. You don't have to do that. I've survived on my own for a while, so I can figure things out for myself. I'll go check on it," Camille said, quickly standing from her chair.

Leah threw a sharp look at Vincent and asked Camille bluntly, "How long has it been since your husband passed away?"

Camille raised an eyebrow and pressed her lips tightly together before responding, "My Robert is still alive. I told you before, he's on a business trip right now."

"When will he be back?" Leah asked. "Will we get to meet him?"

Camille laughed and tucked her shiny, red hair behind her ears. "*No, no, you won't get to meet him. He'll be back soon, though. After you all are gone.*"

"And when will that be?" Leah continued, trying to extract as much information as she could from the strange writer. Or witch. Whatever she was.

"Soon," Camille promised them. "It will all be over soon."

Chapter 29:
Camille

Leah was sitting awfully close to the fire. Camille jumped up from her armchair, startling Brody to the floor with a yelp. She charged forward and pushed the surprised Leah into the fire with a grunt.

Leah attempted to regain her balance and find safety away from the flames, but it was too late. Camille picked up the fire poker from the stand next to the fireplace and shoved it into the fire before stabbing Leah through the chest and sending her further backward. As her flesh melted, her screams seemed to echo throughout the small room. Her lovely light brown braids shriveled and disintegrated. Her eyes were wild as she clutched at the scorching bricks and scrambled to get out of the fireplace. Vincent darted toward his girlfriend, perhaps reacting slowly from the shock. But it was too late.

Camille watched her burn alive, and a warm glow spread throughout her body. This was what she was meant for—this was her purpose in life. She cackled and stepped back to ensure she didn't catch on fire herself, and then—

"Camille? Camille, are you all right?" a male voice asked. A hand gently shook her in her chair.

Disconcerted, Camille opened her eyes and flinched at the hand touching her, not realizing at first who it was. "Oh, it's you, Vincent."

He peered down at her with his dark eyebrows scrunched together. "You fell asleep while we were hanging out in here. Then it sounded like you were having a bad dream or something. You were thrashing around in the chair and laughing."

Camille smiled and patted her hair self-consciously, certain it was a mess if she had fallen asleep in the armchair. "Ah, yes, just a nightmare. I'm fine."

The thought that Leah and Vincent could have done something to her while she was sleeping crossed her mind, but she wasn't sure if they were capable of anything so heinous.

She was the one who was capable of such things, not them. Even when their lives were at stake, they were both such goody two shoes. Especially Leah. Now, Vincent—Camille could see him killing someone if he had to. If the stakes were high enough. Perhaps if she threatened Leah? Either way, he seemed tough. Like he would do whatever it took to protect Leah.

She couldn't dwell on it, though. She had plans to enact, plans that were already set in motion. The only thing that worried her was being able to write the ending of the novel before they realized what was happening. She still needed enough time to write a few more chapters. They weren't dumb; they suspected Camille had a hand in the situation, but they had no clue how powerful she really was. Her power was nearly Godlike, although she hadn't fully tested her capabilities yet. Maybe if they knew what she could do, then they wouldn't want to upset her. They would be terrified if they knew the truth.

Noah and Ava came into the room, distracting Vincent and Leah momentarily. Camille seized her opportunity.

After trudging over to her desk, Camille pretended to tidy her notes for her novel. Normally, she kept them neatly in file folders, organized so she could easily find what she needed, but that wouldn't do right now. She put the files in a specific order and slid them back into the folder when Leah moved toward her desk.

"What's up?" Leah asked curiously, peering at the desk.

"Just tidying up," Camille said, stacking the papers in the folder and closing it.

"Oh, do you need help with anything?" Leah offered, stepping closer to the desk.

"No, I'll finish up later. I think I'm going to take a shower. My hair is greasy." She ran a hand through her hair. "I'll be out in a jiffy," Camille said, waving goodbye to Leah and the others and then heading toward the master bedroom.

A shower sounded refreshing, and the time to relax in the steaming water would do wonders for her aching back and shoulders. As much as she tried to convince herself she wasn't aging, of course she was, and sleeping on the couch didn't help her back issues. Years of writing and sitting in front of a desk for hours on end had wreaked havoc on her body.

While she was in the shower, enjoying the hot water scalding her skin and temporarily providing relief to her aches and pains, she reminisced about when Robert used to give her a massage after a particularly long writing session. He had always known just how much pressure to apply to make her body feel better. Plus, he knew she was more likely to want sex after a nice massage. She sighed, missing Robert and wishing he was in Japan on a business trip. That he would return home soon. Back to her, his beloved wife.

Oh, how she wished that was the truth, and not that she had buried him underneath the garden in the yard.

Chapter 30: Leah

"Look at all these papers on Camille's desk." Leah beckoned the others over while Camille was gone.

As soon as she heard the water running in the bathroom, she had run over to Camille's desk to see what she had been doing before she left the room. It might be the only time they had to check out her desk and read her files for clues about what she was up to. She never seemed to leave them alone in this room. Probably for a reason. She was clearly hiding something.

Ava hesitated near the couch, not stepping any closer to the desk. Her hands fluttered aimlessly, as if she didn't know what to do with them. "Isn't that, like, rude to snoop through her things?"

Vincent laughed and joined Leah by the desk. "I'm pretty sure Camille is trying to trap us here forever and make sure we can't leave. Don't you think that warrants us snooping? Aren't you curious about what she wants from us?"

"Um, not really. I'm scared to find out," Ava said softly, tugging on the ends of her platinum hair.

Noah boldly strode over to the desk and stood next to Leah and Vincent. "Well, I want to know, so I'll find out for both of us."

Leah opened the folder and began reading the first document before dread settled in her stomach, heavy enough to weigh her down to the bottom of the ocean.

Character Profiles

Vincent Pierce: 18-year-old male. High school graduate. Only child. Enjoys hiking, camping, and outdoor activities. He has been dating Leah for two years. He is from Michigan and has lived there his entire life. When he was young, his mom left him and his dad. His dad raised him as a single father, and they were very close. Vincent tells people his mom abandoned him because she was a terrible parent who never wanted kids. This is partially true, but not the entire truth...

"Vincent, this page is titled *character profiles*. The first one is all about you." Leah continued reading and stopped to flip over the first page. "Oh my God."

"What?" Vincent hurried forward to read whatever Leah had discovered. "It's about me? Why is she writing about me?" Vincent snatched the paper from Leah's hand and read it.

Leah stared at him, waiting to see his reaction.

"It's not all true, is it, Vince? How does she know so much about you?" Leah asked, her stomach becoming queasy in a different way than it had the night before when she drank too much.

This time, she was uneasy with the potential scenarios that had led to Camille knowing most of Vincent's life story. Had he been talking to her when she was out of the room? Had they become so close that he disclosed his deepest, darkest secrets to her?

"It's... mostly true. You know about my mom leaving my dad and I when I was little, and that my dad raised me by himself. We were close and his death..." He stopped talking, becoming choked up at the mention of his dad's death. His warm brown eyes brimmed with tears and he stared at the ground, unable to continue speaking.

"It's okay. I don't want you to relive painful memories, but..." Leah hesitated before venturing to ask the question pounding around in her head after reading the notes in the file. "Is the rest of it true?"

"What does it say?" Noah asked curiously, reaching forward to grab the paper from Vincent's hand.

Vincent yanked his hand away before Noah could grab the paper. "It doesn't matter. It's not important." He closed the folder and kept the paper clutched in his hand. "Ava's right. We shouldn't be snooping around in Camille's things. It isn't right. This is private information."

"But, Vince, she—" Leah protested.

Vincent firmly shook his head. "I know what I said before, but these are just notes about that book she's writing. This has nothing to do with us or what she's doing to us."

"Then why is your name on there? How does she know about—" Leah asked.

"I don't know how she knows so much about me, but we'll find out another way. Besides, not all of this is true, only parts of it. I don't know how she found out so much about me," Vincent said in a frosty tone.

"Oh my God, has she been following us or keeping tabs on us somehow? Even before we stumbled across her cabin?" Ava said. Her hands went to her mouth, and she gasped in terror.

"But why would she do that? What does she want from us?" Noah questioned.

"And how did she know we would come here?" Leah asked, playing with her braids, making sure her hair was still tidy and no strands were out of place.

Vincent chewed on his bottom lip, appearing thoughtful. Leah had never seen him look so scared.

"We need to confront her and ask her where she got this information about us," Vincent said.

"Is that smart, considering everything she's done to us?" Leah placed her hand on Vincent's shoulder, darting another glance at the paper in his hand. "Are you sure we should bring it up to her?"

"It's our only option. We're stuck here with her, so we might as well find out the truth," Vincent whispered. "When she gets out of the shower, we'll talk to her. We need answers. This will help us get out of here."

Leah sighed, not wanting to go against her boyfriend's wishes, but also wanting to know if what it said in the character profile with Vincent Pierce's name in front of it was all true. And if it was, why had Vincent lied to her? It was a huge thing to lie about something that had affected the way he grew up, his childhood, and how he was raised. Maybe it even had something to do with the reason he didn't want kids. If his mom had left for such a terrible thing, then some things Leah had never understood about Vincent made sense. She only needed to find out how much of it was true. She knew he was hiding something from her.

After Vincent had placed the files back in the folder and tried to arrange everything as they had found it, they all headed back to the couch and sat down, impatiently waiting for Camille to finish her shower and come back out to the main room. She seemed to take an exceedingly long time, but she finally returned with her curly, red hair blow-dried, wearing a flannel shirt and jeans.

"Hello," Camille said, taking her seat in the armchair. "What's going on?" she asked, peering at the group silently huddled together on the couch.

"How do you know all those things about me?" Vincent blurted out, unable to contain himself or ease their questions into the conversation more naturally.

A wicked smile crept across Camille's face. "Did you go through my things, Vincent?"

Vincent gulped, glancing down at the wooden floor for a few seconds before gathering his courage and making eye contact with Camille. "Yeah, I know it was disrespectful, but we wanted to find out some things. We saw the character profile for Vincent Pierce. Is that about me?"

Camille cocked her head slightly and appraised him. "Wouldn't you be the best person to answer that? If it is about you, wouldn't you be able to tell?" Camille glanced at Leah. "Does she know the truth about what your mother did?" she asked, inclining her head toward Leah.

Vincent stood from the couch, clenching his fists at his sides. "It's not true what you wrote in there! That's *not* how it happened. My mom left my dad and I. She abandoned us, but not because of..." He fell backward onto the couch, putting his head in his hands and attempting to stifle his sobs.

Leah couldn't remember Vincent ever crying in front of her or becoming so emotional, except on the day of his dad's funeral. Besides that, he wasn't the type of person to blatantly display his emotions, especially in front of other people, and when one of them was basically a stranger. She instinctively reached for him, placing her hand on his back and rubbing in circles to soothe him.

"It's okay, Vince," she whispered. "You can tell me the truth."

Eventually, he looked up at her, blinking as more tears fell down his cheeks. "I can't," he said hoarsely. "I can't tell you what really happened."

Chapter 31: Camille

"Do you two want a minute to talk alone? You're welcome to use the guest bedroom for some privacy." She pointed toward the hallway.

Vincent vehemently shook his head, refusing to be alone with Leah. It seemed like, despite the obvious evidence of the horror of what his mom had done, he was insistent on denying it and acting like it was a lie. He couldn't even trust his girlfriend of over two years with the truth. Why was that? Was it shame, fear, or something else holding him back from telling her his deepest, darkest secret?

Leah turned to Vincent, trying to catch his attention, but he refused to make eye contact with her.

"Vince? Come on, let's go talk in private, and you can tell me what's going on. You don't have to say it in front of everyone else if you don't want to." She placed her hand on his arm in what she probably thought was a reassuring manner, but Vincent immediately shook her hand off.

"Stop. I already told you it's not true, so there's nothing to talk about," Vincent said harshly, backing away from her.

Leah stared at her boyfriend as if she couldn't believe how Vincent had reacted. She retreated into the hallway. "I'll be in the spare bedroom if you change your mind," she said.

Ava narrowed her dark brown eyes at Vincent, her perfectly manicured eyebrows squishing together as she did so, and stepped toward him. "Are you that much of an idiot? Don't just let her go sit in there by herself. Go talk to her and tell her the truth." She nudged Vincent, but he didn't budge.

Instead, he crossed his arms over his chest and leaned back into the couch, settling in. "There's nothing to talk about," he said again stubbornly. "None of it's true."

Ava rubbed her eyes. "None of it? Some of it is definitely true, which I think is why Leah is questioning the parts you're denying."

Noah wrapped his arm loosely around Ava's shoulders. "Babe, chill. Just let him be. If he doesn't want to talk about his past, then he doesn't have to."

"Thanks, man," Vincent said.

"I mean," Noah continued, "you might lose Leah over it, and she's probably the best thing to happen to you, but who am I to tell you that you're making the wrong decision? It's your choice how you deal with it."

Vincent sighed, seeming to deflate somewhat. He uncrossed his arms and balled his fists at his sides. "I don't want to lose her."

Camille spoke up. "It's probably best to talk to her, Vincent. Just be honest with her. Honesty is always the right decision. If she judges you for whatever you tell her, then it's not meant to be. You deserve someone who accepts you, faults, messy past, and all."

Vincent pulled the elastic from his hair, undid the ponytail, gathered all his hair up in his hands, made sure it was tightly together and no strands of hair were astray, then redid the ponytail, pulling on the elastic after to make sure it was tight enough. Camille watched him do it, assuming it was a nervous habit.

Why was he so nervous about speaking with Leah if she was the woman he loved, the one he planned to be with forever? Weren't the people who loved you supposed to love you no matter what? Otherwise, what was the point? If it could all crumble with one lie, a hidden, tragic history, or in her case, an obsession with the books she wrote?

"You're going to let us leave," Vincent said, pointing at Camille. "But first, you're going to tell us what's really going on here."

Camille chuckled and tucked her curly red hair behind her ears. "What do you mean?"

"You know what's happening to us. I don't know how you learned so much about us, if it's magic or witchcraft or something else. But you manipulated us, somehow made us find your cabin, you did something to the tow truck, you made the windows disappear, and the door can't be unlocked... all things that should be impossible because they defy logic. Yet you somehow made them happen. How did you do it, Camille? And better yet, why us? *Why are you torturing us?*" Vincent became louder as he kept talking, "Why won't you let us leave?"

Camille sat firmly in her armchair, unmoving, then crossed one leg over the other, folding her hands in her lap. She needed to appear to the others for all intents and purposes as if she was a polite woman, simply a writer living alone in a cabin in the woods with her dog and her husband away on a business trip, soon to return to her. But that wasn't the truth at all.

She was so much more than that. Part of her yearned for them to know the truth, to understand the magnitude of what she had done. To feel struck with fear at how much power she possessed, that she could manipulate them and make them do things they didn't want to do.

"Vincent, haven't you figured it out by now? You don't strike me as a dumb person. If anyone can figure out what's happening, it's you," Camille said, stroking his ego. She knew it was the surest way to get him to analyze everything in a clear and calm manner, and perhaps he would soon figure it out.

Vincent eyed her and sighed heavily. "All right, fine. If you won't tell us, then I'll guess. You clearly have some way of manipulating us. You don't want us to leave. Camille, you know things about us, even things other people don't know. Have you been stalking us?"

Camille shook her head with a half-smile, and her curls bounced around her shoulders. "How would I have done that from here? I've been in this cabin for months. The four of you live in Michigan. That's a long drive. Didn't you say it's over ten hours from here?"

"Right. But you could be lying," Ava interjected.

Camille snorted. "Do I strike you as the stalker type?"

Ava opened her mouth as if she was about to reply 'yes,' but Noah shushed her.

"No, that's not right," Vincent said. "Too many issues with the stalker angle. It pains me greatly to even suggest this, but I think there's something supernatural going on." He stared at Camille, perhaps waiting for her to confirm or deny his idea.

She didn't do anything to indicate either way.

"The only question is... What type of supernatural powers are we dealing with?" Vincent asked.

Chapter 32: Leah

While Leah waited in the spare bedroom for Vincent to come to his senses, she lay on the bed, staring up at the ceiling. Parts of it were more worn than others, and the off-white paint was chipped and flaking off in some areas. She rested her arms behind her head, wondering what was going on in the main room. What were they talking about? And what did the others think about Vincent not following her to talk?

Leah supposed Ava would gloat about it because she had always been jealous of Leah for having such a great boyfriend. Until this trip, Leah had thought Vincent was basically perfect. Since the snowstorm, howeverer, she realized he wasn't perfect at all. But perhaps that was her fault for having such high expectations for him. She pushed him too much. If he came to talk to her, she would apologize and try to be a better girlfriend. Leah wouldn't leave the room unless he told her about his past. That was for sure.

It's not like she was asking too much of him, though. All she wanted to know was what really happened to his parents. Vincent had never gone into details about his mom leaving, only saying that she abandoned him and his dad when he was in elementary school. He had made it clear he hated her, and Leah had never pushed him to tell her more. She figured it was painful for him to talk about, and she didn't want to force him to relive his most painful memories.

But she wondered if his reasons for not wanting to talk about his mom were entirely different from what she had assumed. Maybe he was ashamed to tell everyone about the awful things written about his mom in the character profile. If it was true, then she could almost understand why Vincent had hidden it from her. But how was she supposed to trust him if he didn't tell her the truth?

As Leah adjusted her position on the bed again and rearranged the pillows to make herself more comfortable, settling in for a long wait, a knock sounded on the door.

"Come in," she yelled.

A tidy, dark brown ponytail appeared. Vincent. "Hey," he mumbled, closing the door behind him and stepping into the room. He tugged on his ponytail like he always did when he was anxious and sat on the edge of the bed.

"Hi," she said, sitting up and leaning back against the headboard. She remained in the same spot, not wanting to frighten him off by getting too close or accidentally accusing him of anything.

Leah waited, expecting Vincent to apologize for how he had acted and tell her the truth about his mom. He did neither of those things.

After a minute, she peered at him with her blue eyes wide behind her glasses and said, "Are you just going to sit there in silence or can we talk?"

"No. We can talk." Vincent sighed, rubbing a hand over his face and then letting it fall back to his side. "This is hard for me to talk about. I've never told anyone the whole truth. The only people who know are my parents, me, and one other person. The whole town thinks they know what happened, but it's only one version of it, not the whole thing."

Now Leah was even more curious.

"Okay, you already know my mom left my dad and I when I was just a kid, but you don't know why."

"I assumed she didn't want kids or wasn't fit to be a parent. That happens to lots of people who accidentally become parents and have to deal with the consequences of an unplanned pregnancy," Leah whispered.

"Yeah, well, it wasn't like that with my mom. She wanted kids, and she always wanted to be a mom. In fact, she loved kids so much that she became a high school English teacher."

"Really? Wow. That's not what I imagined based on what you told me about her." Leah's eyes widened at the revelation.

"I know." Vincent fidgeted with the quilt on the bed, twisting it between his fingers. "My parents' relationship was never that great to begin with, but when my dad started working longer hours and spending more time away from home, my mom was lonely. Every night, when he came home from work, she would yell at him for working too much and said that he wanted to be away from us, but that wasn't true. That's not why he worked so hard. He did it for us, for me, to give me a good life. I don't think she ever understood that."

Unable to resist comforting Vincent, Leah scooted toward him until she was close enough to grab his hand. She entwined their fingers together.

He continued his story, "She kept complaining. They fought more and more over the years, and it affected me. I didn't like being home because they were always arguing. They never became physical with each other, but the verbal fighting was bad enough. Over time, my mom started spending nights away from home. One day, she came home from work early. I think I was about five. A teenager with blond hair to his shoulders came to the door and rang the doorbell, so I answered it. He looked frantic. He asked if my mom was home. I didn't know who he was, but I yelled for her. She came to the door with this haunted expression, looking like someone had just died. A few days later, she was gone. She didn't even say goodbye to me."

Vincent finished, "I was only a kid. I didn't understand what was going on or why my mom had left me. At first, I just wanted her to come home. I remember asking my dad every day when Mom would be home, and he always told me, 'Soon, bud.' I didn't find out until I was older what had really happened and where she went. The real reason she couldn't come home. I wish I had never known what she did. Maybe it would have been easier for me to not know the truth. I've had this secret hanging over me for years. I haven't been able to bring myself to tell anyone." Vincent gulped, and his gaze went to the floor.

"What did she do, Vince?" Leah asked, sure she was missing a crucial piece of the puzzle to figuring out what had happened.

Vincent's face became cold and hard as he made eye contact with her at last. "She slept with one of her students. His parents found out, and they were furious, of course. He tried explaining it wasn't rape because it was consensual, but he was only sixteen. He was still a minor. His parents convinced him to nail her with a rape charge. She was found guilty and sentenced to seven years in prison. My dad was livid about the whole situation, and he didn't take me to see her. He was probably embarrassed too. Everyone in town knew what had happened because it was all over the news. I found out about it later. All the articles about her. 'Local High School English Teacher Sleeps With Student.' That's why my dad decided we should move to the other side of the state. Somewhere no one knew us, so we could have a fresh start."

Vincent paused and bit his lip. "I was young, and I didn't know what my mom had done, but all I wanted was to see her. Now that my dad's gone, I feel guilty about how I treated him when my mom left. It wasn't fair to him. I know I was only five, but I just wanted my mom back and for us to be a happy family again. My dad must have been going through so much. He never gave up on me, though. He tried his best to be a good dad." Vincent sniffled and wiped his nose with the sleeve of his hoodie.

"Did you ever go see your mom after you found out the truth?" Leah asked, squeezing his hand.

He squeezed her hand back. "Yeah, I went to see her when I turned eighteen. She was out of prison by then, but my dad had forced her to sign a contract saying she wouldn't try contacting me until I was an adult and could decide for myself whether I wanted to see her. At that point, I had so many questions for her, but mostly, I was mad about what she did to our family. Now, I realize if she and my dad had stayed married, we all would have been miserable. At least I grew up being raised by a caring dad who tried his best to give me a good life." Vincent sniffled again, his eyes turning red and watery. "When I saw her, she asked if I wanted to meet her husband. I said sure, with no clue about what was about to happen. The guy walked out of the kitchen and waved to me. He smiled this shit-eating grin and asked if I remembered him. It was the blond teenager, her former student she had slept with. Apparently, they stayed in contact while she was in prison. She went back to him when her sentence was up, and he waited all those years for her. Last I heard, they had two kids together, so I guess I have two half-brothers. I've never met them, though." His body drooped as he finished the story.

"Wow," was all Leah could muster. "That's like something in a movie. I'm really sorry, Vince. I had no idea." She leaned in close to him and rested her head on his shoulder, looking up at him with sympathy.

"It's fine. It's my fault for not telling you sooner. I never meant to hide things from you, but as time passed, and I still hadn't told you about my mom, I couldn't make myself do it. And then, my dad died. I didn't want to relive the entire awful scenario again when I was already going through something terrible. It was too hard to tell you. I didn't know what you would think when you found out. I worried you would think less of me, and I couldn't bear it."

"Vince, I'm sorry you went through all that, but it's not your fault. You were only a kid, and there's nothing you could have done," she whispered, kissing his cheek. "I'm here for you, no matter what."

"Thanks." Vincent wrapped his arms around her and hugged her tightly. "Just so you know, if your mom slept with a minor and went to prison or something crazy like that, now is the time to tell me," he said with an awkward laugh.

"Nope." Leah shook her head playfully. "Sorry, my family is completely normal compared to yours."

He hit her gently on the shoulder before pulling her close to him for another hug.

"There is something I have to tell you, though."

Vincent let go of her and pulled back to meet her eyes. "Okay, what is it?"

Leah took a deep breath. It wasn't as bad as his revelation, so she could do this. She could finally tell him the truth. "I didn't get into Michigan State. I lied to everyone about the acceptance letter. I was rejected. I was so sure I would get in that I only applied to one other school, and now I don't know what to do. My future is ruined." Tears formed in her eyes and threatened to fall. She hastily wiped them away before they could fog up her glasses.

Vincent reached forward to brush a stubborn tear from her cheek. "Hey, it's okay. It's not the end of the world. My life isn't turning out anything like I thought it would. The important thing is we have each other. We'll figure out the whole college thing when we get home."

Leah leaned into his chest and put her head on his shoulder. "You mean, *if* we ever get home." She sniffed and rubbed her nose.

"Yeah, we need to figure out how the hell to get out of this cabin."

"I know," Leah replied, her playful attitude diminishing as she remembered the dire situation they were in. It seemed impossible.

But she had Vincent by her side once again, and there weren't any secrets between them. So, at least for the moment, she could almost pretend all was right with the world and that there weren't dangerous forces at work, preventing them from escaping their prison in a small cabin in the woods.

Chapter 33: Camille

After what seemed like an eternity to the anxious Camille, Vincent emerged from the spare bedroom with Leah, hand in hand. It appeared they had resolved things. Camille wondered if Vincent had told Leah everything.

She eyed their entwined fingers. Well, if he did, then Leah seemed to be okay with it. Camille frowned, the creases deepening in her face. That wasn't how it was supposed to happen. The truth should have disgusted and outraged Leah. Vincent had lied to her for two years about why his mom had left. He had withheld important information about his past. But Leah had just forgiven him so easily?

"Is everything okay?" Ava rose from her spot on the couch next to Noah and moved toward her sister. She looked at Leah and Vincent, perhaps searching for a clue as to what had transpired in the spare bedroom.

Leah smiled at Vincent, clearly delighted with him. "Yes, everything is fine. You don't have to tell them what you told me if you don't want to," she added to Vincent, tugging on his ponytail. "I promise I'll keep your secret."

"Thanks, sweetie," Vincent answered as he led her over to the couch.

Ava joined them on the couch, seeming satisfied with the outcome, and they all lapsed into silence.

No one prompted Vincent to spill whatever he had told Leah. Camille's mind raced. She needed to shake things up again. She wanted to terrify them, make them believe they wouldn't get out of her cabin alive. And they still might not. She hadn't decided yet. Sometimes it was fun to make a spur-of-the-moment decision. Let the chips fall where they may...

"Since that's all out of the way, what are your plans for the rest of the day?" Vincent asked, still holding Leah's hand but now sitting beside her on the couch.

He was addressing her, Camille realized, and asking what her plans were.

His question had thrown her off, but she didn't want any of them to know that. She was supposed to be the one in control. They still hadn't uncovered the source of her power, and she wasn't sure she wanted them to. They would only use it against her. Or figure out a way to steal it and use it for themselves. She couldn't have that happen. Things were already going off the rails, and she didn't want the game to be over yet. She thought quickly.

"How about I make a nice, big lunch for us? No one ate breakfast, and I'm sure everyone is hungry now," Camille offered, smiling innocently.

There. No one could argue with being fed. Especially teenagers who seemed to eat constantly.

To her surprise, however, Leah piped up, "No thanks, we're fine."

Vincent agreed with her, and after several unsure sideways glances without words being exchanged, Ava and Noah said they weren't hungry, either. Bewilderment flickered over Camille. She hadn't expected them to turn down food.

"Surely, you're hungry? You haven't eaten all day. I don't mind sharing my food with you. I enjoy cooking for other people. It's one of my favorite hobbies," Camille persisted.

"That's okay. We'll just stop at a restaurant or something when we're on the road," Vincent said with a shrug.

Camille raised an eyebrow inquisitively. "On the road?" she repeated.

Leah nodded. "Now that we know how to leave, we'll be going soon." She gestured to Ava and Noah, lifting her hand up.

They obediently stood from the couch, although they most likely didn't know all the details Leah and Vincent had figured out. How could they, since they had been out here while Leah and Vincent talked in the bedroom?

Quickly, Camille scrambled to her feet as well. What was happening? This wasn't part of her plan. This wasn't how it was supposed to go! She never should have let Leah and Vincent be alone together. They were ruining everything.

Her eyes narrowed. Wait a second. This wasn't right. They must be lying. They were trying to trick her into saying something that would help them. Well, she was far smarter than them and had about two decades on them in years, so she would still win this battle.

"How are you planning on doing that?" she asked.

Leah shrugged one shoulder, further irritating Camille. These young people and their nonchalant expressions of indifference. They could never make up their minds.

"You have a plan, *don't you*?" Camille asked with a hand on her hip.

Leah glanced at Vincent, who smiled at her encouragingly. She took a deep breath and expelled it. "Yes, we do, but I won't tell you about it. Thanks *so much* for your hospitality, Camille," she said sarcastically, "but we're leaving now."

"Not so fast," Camille said, moving to stand in front of the fireplace.

The fire was burning low, but they couldn't leave as long as it was still burning. She assumed the fireplace was their escape plan. They hadn't been able to come up with anything else earlier, as far as she knew. And there wasn't another way out. There's no way she could have missed anything.

Camille reached for the small pile of logs next to the fireplace poker and other tools and arranged two more logs in the fireplace. She made sure they both caught on fire before stepping back and wiping off her hands on her pants.

There. That should do it. She stood in front of the roaring fire, blocking their only exit, daring them to defy her.

Chapter 34: Leah

Before Leah and Vincent had left the spare bedroom, they had planned an escape. They speculated about what was going on and thought back through everything that had happened to them since meeting Camille.

First, Vincent brought up the fact that Camille had placed nuts on the table when they first arrived, somehow expecting Leah's nut allergy. Another day, she had brought out wine and poured generous glasses for all of them, revealing Ava's struggle with drinking after Ava refused a glass. Both times Camille reacted erratically—throwing out all the food potentially 'contaminated' by the nuts and dumping out the bottle of wine.

As they talked, they both realized every time they ate something Camille had cooked, they began hallucinating or feeling sick. The packaged goods hadn't seemed to affect them, so they thought Camille had been putting something in the food she cooked to drug them.

Vincent had also discovered that Camille knew his darkest secret—the truth about his mom sleeping with one of her students and going to prison. The only way she could have found that out was if she had been stalking them or if there were other nefarious powers at work that she had control over. All of this added up to mean one thing.

They needed to get the hell out of this cabin.

It seemed like Camille had done everything in her power to lure them there and torture them, and she didn't intend on letting them leave.

The next time Camille left the room, whether it was to go to the bathroom or the kitchen, one of them would immediately dash for Camille's desk and skim through the other files in her folder. Vincent was sure the answers were in there, and Leah agreed with him.

That had been where they found out she knew Vincent's entire background and life story. Did she know just as much about the rest of them? If so, maybe her plans for them were in the folder too. Reading the files was their best shot at figuring out how to get out of the cabin, but first, they needed to convince Camille that they already had a foolproof escape plan. Then they needed to distract her, so they could figure out how to leave.

Leah didn't think Camille would take kindly to her 'guests' trying to leave and not viewing her as hospitable anymore. She was sure Camille would crack if she thought they had found a way out, because that would mean she was no longer in control, something she clearly obsessed over.

After Camille threw several more logs on the fire and ensured it was roaring steadily again, she stood in front of the fireplace, assuming their plan had been an escape through the chimney, like they had talked about previously. It was a smart move, but it wasn't their plan.

Leah eyed the axe near the fireplace, noting that it was still next to the fire poker and other tools. She just needed to get to it without making it obvious what she was doing. She needed to make Camille leave the room.

"I thought I was fine, but I'm suddenly feeling pretty hungry," Leah announced. "Anyone else?"

"Me too," Noah chimed in, patting his stomach.

Camille looked at her with her green eyes narrowed to slits.

Shit. Is she going to believe me?

"All right, I can whip something up for everyone," Camille offered, moving away from the fireplace. "I'll be right back."

When Camille went into the kitchen, Vincent darted for Camille's desk, and Leah went toward the axe. Noah and Ava stared at them in confusion and stood by the couch, unmoving. When Vincent and Leah both ran across the room, Brody jumped up from his resting place in Camille's armchair and started barking at them.

From the kitchen, Camille yelled, "Everything all right in there?"

"Yup, fine. Just playing with Brody!" Vincent answered quickly.

"So, what's the plan?" Noah asked.

"What's going on?" Ava said.

Leah picked up the axe and carried it to where Noah and Ava stood in front of the couch. She handed it to Noah. "This is our best weapon. We also have the homemade pepper spray and the flamethrower, but I think you'll be the best with the axe. Vincent is looking through Camille's files to see if there's anything in there that can help us."

"Why do we need these weapons?" Ava chewed her bottom lip and eyed the axe.

Noah slowly nodded in understanding. "To fight Camille if she tries to hurt us." He placed his hand firmly around the handle of the axe. "Don't worry, Camille doesn't stand a chance against us. There are four of us and only one of her."

"Yeah, but we still don't know what we're up against," Ava said, standing behind Noah and wrapping her arms around his waist. "She could be more powerful than all of us if she's really a witch."

"Have you found anything, Vince? Do you know what she's planning next?" Leah turned to face her boyfriend, who sat hunched over the pieces of paper on the desk.

Vincent was quiet for a few seconds before he held up a sheet of paper that only had two words written on it.

In all capital letters, the words 'KILL VINCENT' were scrawled across the page in sloppy handwriting.

"Guys, I think Camille is coming after me first."

Chapter 35: Camille

When Camille reentered the main room of the cabin, holding a tray full of food, shock sizzled through her as she saw her guests all sitting calmly on the couch, chatting and laughing amongst themselves. A small part of her had thought they were planning something like a coup and that they would attack her as soon as she was back in the room. She thought they had wanted to get her out of the room so they could talk without her listening and formulate an escape plan. Well, she wouldn't let them be alone again. She wouldn't leave the room for anything. They could fetch their own darn food next time.

Camille set the loaded tray on the coffee table, displaying an assortment of snacks, similar to what she had provided on their first day at her cabin. She hoped they noticed and that the irony wasn't lost on them. Maybe this would be their last day with her. It all depended on how this next part went.

If they tried anything, she was ready to end it.

"Bon appétit," she said with a flourish of her hand and a smile at her guests. She picked up a few crackers and nibbled on them, then sipped from her mug of hot chocolate she had left on the table earlier.

"Thanks, Camille," they each muttered in what sounded like an unappreciative tone to the suspicious Camille.

One by one, they picked up the food and ate.

Camille smiled, keeping up her persona of being unaware that they had something planned. She was certain they did. But as long as they all ate the truffles, everything would work out perfectly fine. She assumed they would because who didn't like chocolate truffles? Only psychopaths and serial killers, that's who. Probably rapists too.

However, as each of them finished up their snacking, Camille realized all twelve truffles were still sitting on the tray, patiently waiting their turn to be chosen. She frowned and quickly discarded the unhappy look. She didn't want to appear out of sorts, but she was feeling unnaturally sleepy.

Camille stifled a yawn and pointed to the truffles. "Oh, these truffles are marvelous!" she exaggerated, slightly staggering on her feet. She gripped the edge of the coffee table so she didn't fall over. "Robert brought them back for me from France. You can't find chocolate like this in the United States. It just doesn't taste the same. Help yourselves!"

"We wouldn't want to eat your *special* chocolates, Camille," Vincent said, emphasizing the word special and looking directly at her. "Those are reserved just for you."

What? Did he know her secret? But how could he?

She had taken such care to make sure no one noticed.

By the time Camille could grasp the fact that they had fooled her, she stumbled back to her armchair, barely collapsing into the chair before she lost consciousness.

***

Brody barked, shocking Camille out of her forced slumber. Groggily, she awoke, darting her eyes around to find her precious dog. Surely, they wouldn't hurt an animal!

With relief, she spotted him sitting in front of her on the floor, barking at her expectantly. He had probably been worried when she fell unconscious. She sighed, thankful her little Brody was all right. After she lost Robert, Brody was all she had, and she couldn't bear the thought of anything happening to him.

Camille made her best attempt to get to her feet, at first wondering why she couldn't get up. Then, when her eyes shifted down, she saw a thick rope binding her arms around the chair. She was no longer in her favorite armchair. She was sitting in one of the wooden chairs from the kitchen. Brody was too far away for her to reassure him that she was fine, so his anxious barking continued. And worse yet, she was trapped.

She turned her gaze to the couch diagonal from her chair and made eye contact with Vincent. "You spiked my drink. How could you?" she asked him in a soft tone, astonished that after everything she had done for him and his friends, he had betrayed her in the end. At one point, Camille had thought they would be together, but that hope was dashed to smithereens now.

Vincent smiled cheekily, his ponytail swishing back and forth in perfection. "Oh, Camille, didn't you see this coming? I thought you knew what would happen. We learned from you, after all." He held up the piece of paper that said 'KILL VINCENT' on it. "What did you expect after we found this? For us to be best friends and want to live here with you forever?"

Camille sniffed self-consciously and turned her nose up at them. "I was only trying to—"

"What? Kill me?" Vincent said, waving the piece of paper back and forth to emphasize his words. "Why?"

She shook her head, straining against the rope and doing her best to loosen it, but it was no use. The knots were too tight. She would have to talk her way out of this one.

Camille hung her head in resignation for a moment, saying a silent prayer for forgiveness for what she was about to do. "Okay, Vince. I'll tell you everything."

Chapter 36: Leah

Leah didn't believe Camille for one second. She was playing them, hoping they would untie her so she could continue toying with them in whatever sick game she was playing. She stared at Camille unflinchingly, hoping Vincent and the others were on the same page as her. There was no way anyone believed Camille's act.

"Stop fighting against the rope. You won't be able to get out of it without our help. Vince was a Boy Scout for years, and he used to go camping with his dad all the time. He's an expert at tying knots," Leah said, keeping her distance from Camille in case she tried something.

Although they had tied Camille up, they didn't know what she was capable of. If she was a witch, maybe she could use magic to break free from the rope. Although Leah hadn't seen a wand or any magical tools anywhere... Unless she had hidden her witchy things?

"Don't you think I already know all that?" Camille spat, straining against the rope. "I know everything about you. I know all of your secrets. Even the worst things you've done that you don't want anyone to know."

Leah gulped, swallowing down her nerves. They had suspected Camille knew more than she had let on about them, but to hear her say it out loud was eerie. No one expected a stranger to know intimate details about their life without telling them.

"How?" Leah asked. Her brow furrowed as she pondered the possibilities. None of this made sense.

Camille tried to adjust her position in the wooden chair, but she wasn't able to move much because of the rope. She sighed and stopped struggling.

"Prove it," Vincent said, standing bravely in front of Camille, with his arms hanging by his sides. "Prove you know something about one of us no one else would know."

A sinister smile crept across Camille's pretty face like a shadow. "All righty then. Noah read Ava's diary when he was at her house last year. He's the one who told Ava's parents about her drinking problem and suggested she needed help."

Noah's mouth dropped open at the revelation. He stuttered, "That's... How did you... It's not like I was snooping..."

Ava turned to her boyfriend. Her reaction surprised Leah. She smiled fondly as she said, "I don't see that as a bad thing. You were concerned about me, and you're the reason I could finally ask for help. I was too scared to tell anyone how bad the drinking had gotten. I didn't know what to do. You helped me find a way out of it." She kissed Noah on the cheek.

Noah closed his eyes briefly. When he opened them, he put his arm around Ava. "Of course. I only wanted to help you. I realize I invaded your privacy, but I was so worried. Sorry for reading your diary, though. That was the only time I ever did it, I swear."

Vincent turned back to Camille again. "You could have guessed that. That proves nothing. Tell us something really awful."

Leah tugged on Vincent's arm. "Vince, stop. We don't need to do this."

"Fine, if you insist," Camille replied with a heavy sigh. "I'm the reason your father committed suicide."

Vincent's eyes seemed to bulge. He took several steps backward, away from Camille. "That's not true. He was troubled, and he hid it from everyone. You didn't even know him."

"Oh, but I did. It's my fault he's dead."

Vincent lunged toward Camille with a snarl. Noah reacted quickly, jumping forward to hold him back.

"Stop, Vincent! This won't help anything. She's just messing with us," Noah insisted. He pinned Vincent's arms back so he couldn't move. Noah was an athlete, so Vincent was no match for him.

"Please tell us why you did this to us," Ava interjected, stepping closer to Camille to plead with her. "We just want to understand, then we'll untie you and leave."

"*I'm the writer*. You have to do what I say!" Camille screamed, her face suddenly turning red and contorting into fury.

Ava backed away at Camille's outburst. Noah let go of Vincent to stand by her protectively.

Vincent stepped toward Camille again. Leah worried about what he would do. She reached out for his hand, but he pushed her away.

Biting her lip, Leah stood beside Vincent as he questioned Camille.

"Okay, I'll play along. Why did you make my dad commit suicide? And why do you want to kill me? Don't give me that bullshit about us 'finding out when the time is right' or whatever else you're going to say as an excuse. We want the truth," Vincent demanded.

"No. Swearing. In. My. Home," Camille said, forcing each word out. She glared at Vincent with venom in her cool, green eyes.

Vincent crossed his arms over his chest and stood in front of Camille. "I know you're used to being the one in charge, but that's over now. You're tied up, and if we leave, you'll be stuck there. You'll probably starve to death if you don't die from dehydration first." He pointed at Brody. "Or your dog will get so hungry that he'll eat you. Is that what you want?"

Camille sobbed and tried to turn her head to see Brody, who was happily lying in front of the fireplace, his little paws stretched out, enjoying the warmth. "No," she rasped in a barely audible tone.

"Okay, good. Now, why do you want to kill me?" Vincent asked again. He tapped his foot as they all waited with bated breath for her answer.

Camille remained silent, staring Vincent down with a fierce look in her eyes.

"Camille, do you want to die in here? I already warned you—we'll leave you tied up, and you won't have a way to escape. If you don't give us some answers, that's what will happen. You'll die, and your dog will too. I'm not messing around," Vincent threatened, his brown eyes darkening until they were nearly black.

The look on his face terrified Leah. She had never seen him like this. She wasn't sure if Camille was lying, but if she was telling the truth… How had she made Vincent's dad kill himself?

"Fine, I don't suppose I have much of a choice." Camille stared longingly at Vincent, as if she was reminiscing. "You remind me so much of my beloved Robert. I poured him into your character when I created you—"

"Wait. What?" Vincent's voice came out shaky, and his posture stiffened.

The others all snapped their heads toward Camille too.

Camille nodded. "Yes, that's right. That's the truth of how I know so much about you. I know all the intimate details of your lives because I created you."

Chapter 37: Camille

November 1987

Camille drummed her fingers on the steering wheel as classical music drifted through the speakers of her car. She shivered in her long parka and turned up the heat. November in Asheville could be monstrous, and today was a chilly day. Camille was on her way to her cabin with Brody, so she could have some alone time to write. After battling writer's block for months, she needed inspiration. She hoped the beautiful scenery and isolation would help her finish her twentieth novel.

As she drove through the winding mountains, she spotted a sign that said *Yard Sale*. She always loved a good deal. That was how she had furnished both her cabin and regular house. So, she followed the signs. It was a strange time of year for a yard sale. She couldn't remember any houses being out this way. The house had seemed to pop out with no warning, but at least it wasn't snowing.

She parked the car in the driveway and turned to Brody, who was sitting quietly in the passenger seat. "Okay, Brody boy, I'm just going to check this out quickly. I'll be right back. Be good." Camille kissed the top of her dog's head and exited the car.

She didn't see anyone else outside, so she took her time wandering through the items on display. After a while, an inky blackness stole across the sky. As she had just about decided that nothing there was worth her time, she spotted it.

The typewriter sat on a scuffed oak table near the front of the house. It was in pristine condition and appeared brand new, as if it had never been used.

Camille moved closer to the typewriter to inspect it. Maybe a new typewriter was the thing she needed to get her novel going. She rarely treated herself to anything nice, and the typewriter was beautiful. It would be a delightful change to have something new for herself to enjoy.

As Camille wondered if she should knock on the front door of the house, an elderly man came outside with a huge grin. His thick white hair stuck out all around his head from beneath a cowboy hat. He wore a wrinkled plaid shirt and jeans.

"Howdy, missus. You interested in my typewriter?"

"Hello, sir. Yes, I was just looking at it and thinking I might like to buy it. How much is it?" Camille asked, assuming it might be out of her price range. Even though it was a yard sale, the typewriter was in great shape, so surely, he wasn't selling it for cheap.

The man scratched his chin, where white stubble grew in uneven patches. His blue eyes twinkled as he gazed at her. "What do ya plan on doing with it?"

"I'm a writer, and I would love to have a typewriter like that. I'll write my next novel with it," Camille replied, her face practically glowing as she thought about the possibilities.

"A writer? What kinda books do ya write?" He leaned against the table as he spoke to her, crossing his legs.

Camille paused before she answered. People could be so judgmental when they found out what kind of books she wrote. "Murder mysteries."

The man smiled in a friendly manner as he continued asking questions. "What's the next one 'bout?"

"I—I'm afraid I haven't quite decided yet. You see, I've been stuck and I feel as if I'm all out of ideas." Camille gestured to the mountains. "I'm hoping that being up here in my cabin will give me some fresh inspiration. If it doesn't, my agent is probably going to kill me," she added with a mirthless laugh.

"Oh, this'll give you all sorts of good ideas. That's fer sure. I think it's meant to be yours, so I won't charge a penny." He stared at her and waited for her response.

"Wh—what? Oh, no, I couldn't do that to you. You're having a yard sale, so I must give you something." Camille pulled her wallet out of her purse and flipped through it. All that was inside were several old receipts, a tube of ChapStick, and a few single dollar bills. She frowned at the realization that she really was broke. "I'm afraid I don't have much money on me."

"No, no, I don't want yer money."

Camille was taken aback, so she examined the typewriter again. "There isn't something wrong with it, is there?"

The man shook his head and grinned. The wrinkles on his face crinkled with his smile. "Nope, works just fine. Better than fine, in fact."

Camille spotted an inscription on the typewriter and inched her face closer to read it. *Videte omnes qui tenent potestatem clavium, quia potestatem habebunt creandi et destruendi.*

"Is that Latin? What does it mean?" she asked with wonder. She had never seen a typewriter with an inscription like that before.

"Be careful all who wield the power of the keys, for they will possess the power to create and destroy."

"The power to create and destroy," Camille repeated.

Her eyes widened as she stared with longing at the typewriter that she desperately wanted. Something about it called to her. She needed to possess it.

"It's special. The stories ya write on it won't be like anything ye've ever written before. And if ya aren't careful, they might just take over yer life."

Camille touched a few of the keys on the typewriter, making sure none of them were broken or stuck. She couldn't spot any flaws. It was perfect. And she needed it. This was what she had been searching for, the answer to all her problems. This typewriter was special, and it would help her write the best novel she had ever written.

Chapter 38: Camille

Leah was the first one to speak after Camille's story finished. "Are you... You're not saying—"

Camille nodded, and her red curls gleamed in the dim lighting of the cabin. "That's exactly what I'm saying. You're all characters in my book." She stared at Leah with a steely set to her jaw before the next threatening words flew out of her mouth. "Which is why, as soon as I get to my typewriter, I'm going to kill you all."

While Camille explained about her magical typewriter, everyone in the room was so enraptured with her story they hadn't noticed she had loosened the knot on the rope that bound her to the chair.

Vincent may have been a Boy Scout, but his character had been inspired by Robert, her husband who had also loved all things outdoors. He had been an expert in knots and, over the years, he had taught several useful knots to Camille.

One time, she had specifically asked him for a demonstration of how to untie a knot if someone ever kidnapped her. It may have been slight paranoia, but as a woman, you could never be too careful. These sorts of things were important to know. Or maybe it had been a premonition of a circumstance exactly like this one. Whatever the case, Robert had shown her how to tie and untie several types of knots.

When she felt the rope loosen, she realized she could slip free. She only needed to distract them for a little longer, then she could reach her typewriter. The only problem was having enough time to type out deaths for each of them. She would need to be crafty to complete her plan.

Anger rose inside of her at the fact that she hadn't had time to finish the ending of her book sooner. She loved a good plot twist, but that only applied to her books, not real life. She was supposed to be the one writing the plot twists, not living them and dealing with the consequences of an unexpected wrench in her plans.

"What's your plan for getting out of here?" she asked, turning her head to see Vincent.

She assumed he was the one with the plan because he was the smartest and the most logical. The most like her Robert.

"You haven't guessed it by now?" Vincent asked, uncrossing his arms from his chest and stepping even closer to Camille.

Momentarily, she slowed down in loosening the knot, so he wouldn't notice that her arms could slip out of the rope while he was so close to her.

"What?" she asked, willing him to come even closer. His scent of coffee and woodsiness swirled in the air near her, and she nearly swooned.

Vincent moved closer still, and Camille saw her opening. Camille strained forward, slipping out of the rope. She head-butted Vincent. He immediately fell to the floor. He rubbed his head in a daze.

Camille dashed for her desk. The typewriter beckoned to her. But that was when she noticed Vincent had been the distraction the whole time. Ava sat in front of the typewriter, already wildly typing.

Camille moved behind Ava. Before Ava could whirl around and try to stop her, Camille seized hold of Ava's bleached-blonde ponytail. She yanked on it. Hard. Ava screamed and tumbled backward out of the chair. Leah rushed toward her sister, but Camille didn't have time to think. She needed to write. All she needed was a minute of typing to fix this.

As soon as her butt hit the chair, her fingers darted expertly across the keys. Her thoughts flowed directly into the words she typed. Camille's eyes didn't leave the keys until she heard a triumphant yelp from across the room. She glanced up to see Noah standing by the front door, unlatching the deadbolt.

NO! How was it possible for him to unlock the door?

Camille pulled the piece of paper that Ava had been typing on from the typewriter. Ava hadn't needed long to create an escape route. She had typed:

The deadbolt to the front door reappeared, and Noah unlocked it. Then, the windows in the cabin all reappeared as well, no latches or locks holding them closed. The windows were open, and Ava, Leah, Noah, and Vincent could leave the cab—

Camille was certain Ava would have kept typing if she hadn't viciously grabbed her hair and thrown her out of the chair, but what she had already written was bad enough. Camille needed to correct this before they escaped.

Leah charged toward Camille. She depressed a bottle in front of her face, aiming for her eyes. Camille screamed, holding up a hand as a shield. But her reaction was too late. When her eyes immediately started burning and her vision blurred, she realized it was the pepper spray they had made the other day. She didn't think they would use it on *her*. This wasn't her plan. This wasn't how it was supposed to go.

"You little bitch," Camille hissed, squinting through the haze.

Tears leaked from her scorched eyes and rolled down her cheeks. She quickly racked her mind, trying to remember how to recover from pepper spray in the eyes.

Leah gasped, perhaps shocked at Camille's profanity or at the sight of Camille's bloodshot eyes.

"Quick, Leah, get away from her!" Ava shouted.

Through her blurred sight, Camille could barely make out Ava's attempt to get to her feet again. Camille stumbled as the person she assumed was Leah flew past her, scrambling to put distance between them.

Squinting through her tear-streaked eyes, Camille grasped the desk chair for support and tried to get her bearings. Her eyes felt like they were on fire. It was difficult to open them normally. With a gasp, she closed her eyes for a moment, willing the burning sensation to stop. She opened her eyes again, blinking back the stinging tears cascading down her cheeks.

All right, she needed a plan.

Thank goodness she knew the setup of the room. That would help her find her way to the fireplace. She needed to get her hands on the axe and stop them once and for all. Forget keeping them here with her. They had ruined her plans, and now they needed to pay the price.

Camille heard muffled voices and assumed her guests were whispering to each other and debating what to do next. She couldn't give them time to decide. Crossing the room carefully, she darted over to the fireplace, feeling her way across the room by latching onto the couch, then finally feeling the warm stones above the fireplace. The vague shape of someone next to her appeared, but she couldn't quite tell who it was. Was that a dark ponytail?

"Vincent?" she asked, uncertain, with her arms in front of her.

She strained her eyes, trying to make out the person's features, but it was no use. Her eyes needed more time to recover. She reached for the spot next to the fireplace where she normally kept the fire poker, but her hands swept through the air, coming up empty.

"What?" she exclaimed, startled that things weren't in their proper places.

"Are you looking for this?" asked the male voice next to her, brandishing what she assumed was her axe. She smelled a combination of body odor and, strangely enough, what smelled like sausage. Vincent didn't smell so ghastly, nor was his voice so deep and gruff. It had to be Noah.

"Oh, Camille, the first rule of trying to keep prisoners locked away in your cabin is to make sure you remove anything that can be a weapon. But you didn't! You even helped arm us," Vincent said from close by. "Why would you do that?"

Camille shook her head, confused at the sudden turn of events. "No, this isn't how it's supposed to end. This isn't the ending I wrote!" she exploded, backing away from them.

"I think you forgot about something rather important," Leah interjected, while Camille strained to see her.

"It's a magical typewriter, and you might not have understood all the rules. Once we became alive to you, you were still influencing us whenever you wrote scenes directly involving us, but we have free will. I realized that when I thought back on everything that's happened. We're the ones who tried to leave. We called the towing company and tried to escape through the chimney. Ava refused to drink the wine. You get the idea. You intervened every time and redirected the events the way you wanted them to go, but each time, our free will got in the way. That's the thing about messing with magic; you have to be certain of what you're dealing with. You need to make sure you understand the rules," Leah said.

While Leah was talking, Camille's vision had started to clear up. Her eyesight was far from normal, but she could see enough to know that Noah was holding an axe close to her, and the others had gathered nearby.

"What are you planning to do? Kill me?" She gave a quick bark of indignant laughter. "You can't do that. It's impossible. *You're not real!*"

"Hmm, good point. I'm not sure if we can, but we figured that's our best way of getting rid of you, so we can finally leave. Then we won't have to worry about you coming after us or trapping us here again," Vincent said. "We've had enough of your games."

Noah moved toward her, swinging the axe from side to side as he came closer.

"Wait!" Camille said as inspiration struck her. She saw a way out of this. "If you kill me, you'll die. I'm the writer. You're just characters in my book. I created you on that typewriter"—she pointed in the general direction of the magical instrument—"and that means if I die, then you all die too."

Chapter 39: Leah

Shit. Why hadn't I considered that?

Leah wasn't sure if Camille was lying, but it seemed plausible.

Camille had created them with a magical typewriter, so clearly, logic had gone out the window. Who knew how this worked? What was the range of where they could go? Could they really leave, even if they left Camille here alive? Or would they somehow end up in the cabin again after trying to escape?

Leah's mind scrambled for an answer, but none of it made sense. She couldn't fathom the truth. *I'm not real. Neither is Vince, Ava, Noah, or my parents...*

The thought struck her violently, shattering everything she had thought she knew. Her entire existence—the life she had built for herself—it was all a lie. It was all fabricated from Camille's imagination. That meant Leah had done none of the things she remembered: family vacations, making plans with Vince for their first apartment, meeting Vincent and falling in love, helping Ava through her alcohol dependence and becoming closer than ever... None of her memories were real. They were all invented by Camille. What was the point in trying to leave, then? If she didn't exist, if she didn't have a soul and wasn't a real person, why should she want to leave? What was her purpose?

Why had Camille done this to them? What kind of sick, twisted person did this?

Vincent yelled to her, but she only registered him saying her name. She felt like she was underwater, trying to swim up toward the sky, to break through to the surface and suck in a breath of fresh air, but she couldn't. Her thoughts were suffocating her, tethering her underneath the water as she tried to wrap her mind around the fact that none of them existed. None of it was real.

"Leah?" Vincent said again, this time gently touching her shoulder to bring her back to the present.

She whipped her head around to face him, and tears shined in her bright blue eyes. She gasped as she struggled to breathe. Her hands shook as Vincent softly grabbed her arm. "What?" she finally croaked out, her voice sounding foreign to her own ears.

"Let's get out of here! The door is unlocked!" Vincent said, urgently tugging her toward the front door.

Leah dug her sneakers into the wooden floor and let go of Vincent's hand, making Vincent stop trying to drag her. "No."

"What are you doing, Leah? Let's go!" Vincent said, grabbing her hand and trying to pull her toward the door again.

She dropped her hand from his. "Why?" she asked, looking up at him. More tears glistened on her light eyelashes and threatened to fall.

"What do you mean, 'why?' Camille wants to kill me, which means she probably plans to kill all of us. We aren't safe here!" Vincent insisted as he stared at her.

"I know, but why does it matter? You heard Camille. We aren't real. We're just characters in her book, figments of her imagination that only exist because of a magical typewriter," Leah responded, looking away from Vincent and at Camille, who smiled sinisterly.

A shiver ran down Leah's back, and her skin tingled. She may not be real, but what would Camille do to them if they stayed? Would dying hurt any less if she wasn't real? And what about after death? Would they simply cease to exist? Maybe Vincent was right.

Vincent jumped forward, holding Leah's hands between his own. He squeezed both of her hands before saying, "No, it matters. You know why?" He didn't stop talking or give her a chance to respond. "Because even if we aren't real, I know I love you. Love is real. It's the most real thing there is."

Leah sobbed as his words got through to her, crashing through the water she had felt like she was drowning in. He was right. "I love you," she said, closing the small distance between them and wrapping her arms around him in a hug.

Leah heard a slow clap coming from behind her and whipped around.

"Oh, how touching," Camille said sarcastically. "Too bad you won't be going anywhere. You should have left while you had the chance. Now... you're mine."

Leah swallowed hard, trying to dispel her fear. The terror coursing through her entire body definitely felt real. Vincent ended the hug and moved Leah behind him, so he was in a protective stance in front of her. Leah noted that he still held the makeshift flamethrower in his hands. She assumed he wouldn't use it unless he had to, but desperate times called for desperate measures.

To Leah's surprise, Camille didn't come for her and Vincent. Instead, she charged toward Noah and Ava, throwing everyone off. Camille slammed into Noah, knocking the axe from his hands. Ava lunged for the axe. Camille grabbed her arm, digging her long nails into Ava's exposed skin.

Ava screamed and dropped the axe. "Shit!" She rubbed her arm where Camille's nails had pierced her skin.

"Ava, look out!" Leah and Vincent warned her at the same time.

"NO SWEARING IN MY HOUSE!" Camille bellowed.

Ava ducked just in time, narrowly missing being hit by Camille swinging the axe wildly at her head. Camille's eyes roamed the room, deciding who her first victim would be. She turned toward Noah, who had made it to his feet again. He braced himself for an attack.

Vincent ran to them, igniting the homemade flamethrower. But it was already too late. Camille swung the axe toward Noah. Noah tried to dodge the swing, but the axe lodged itself in his chest. Camille tried to pull it out. Noah let out an ear-piercing scream. Camille hesitated while Ava darted forward.

Leah tried to take stock of the situation, but she was queasy and terrified. Of course, Noah wasn't okay—an axe had gone through his chest.

Camille yanked on the axe again, finally pulling it free from where it had been buried in Noah's chest. A squelching noise sickened her as it came out of his flesh.

While Camille regained her hold on the axe and spun around to face the others, Vincent had gotten the flamethrower to work. He aimed it at Camille. Flames shot out, leaping onto the delusional writer.

Chapter 40: Camille

Camille screamed, full of fury. She stumbled backward. Flames licked across her sweater. She clawed at the flames futilely. Vincent had missed her face. Her chest and stomach had caught fire instead.

Brody ran toward her, barking like mad. He was too little to help. Until now, he had seemed to enjoy having other people around. She tried to lie on the floor, thinking of what she had learned as a child. *Stop, drop, and roll.* But she wasn't able to make it into the right position.

Vincent charged at her with the axe. She attempted to block her face with her hands, but the axe came down on her head. Mercifully, there was only darkness after that.

***

When Camille came to, only a few minutes had passed. Her once-beloved characters huddled in a circle around her desk. It wasn't over yet, though. Camille wouldn't give up that easily. She wasn't sure what would happen to them if she died, but she had thought the fear of not wanting to find out would prevent them from killing her. However, it seemed they didn't care. Or had Vincent merely meant to knock her out and not kill her? And what about Noah? Was he dead?

Camille shook her head, trying to clear the fogginess from her mind. She probably had a concussion. She rubbed her aching head, and with a great struggle, sat up. Then her eyes quickly darted down, as she remembered she had been on fire before blacking out.

Her favorite purple sweater had unraveled in several places. Scorch marks marred the fabric. An intense sensation burned across her chest and stomach, filling her with a pain unlike any she had ever felt before. The flames must have seared her skin, but she didn't want to check and alert the others that she was awake. She would worry about her injuries later.

With dismay, she thought about how she would have to get rid of the sweater. *That's something that even dry cleaning can't fix*, she thought and nearly laughed out loud. *Definitely ruined.*

For now, she only needed to survive.

Camille peered at her desk, squinting her eyes to not give away that she was awake. Vincent appeared to be snooping through her files. Her characters wanted answers and assumed they would find whatever they were searching for in her documents for her book. It might be more than they bargained for, though.

Camille's files were full of secrets—secrets each of them had kept from the others. She had helped reveal some secrets, but not all of them. She still had a few tricks up her sleeve, and she hoped it would prove enough.

Camille would win this. She had to. What was she without her magical typewriter? Just a lonely woman living alone with a dog and trying to earn enough money from her books to survive. That wasn't enough for her. That wasn't the life she had envisioned all those years, while she had slaved away, hunched over her typewriter, writing her books, dreaming of a world where she was famous and her books sold millions of copies. She wanted all of that and more. The typewriter was her key to making that happen. That was what the man at the yard sale had promised her—the life of her dreams. *He promised.* But that world seemed impossibly out of reach now.

As Camille shakily sat up, Brody came running over to her and licked her hand repeatedly, showcasing how anxious he was about her wellbeing. She patted him on the head and reassured him that he was a good boy.

The others realized Camille was no longer unconscious. The axe was in Vincent's hands, and he stalked toward Camille, a grim expression on his face. He stopped in front of her and kneeled to her level, where she was still sitting on the floor.

Camille stared at him, unblinking and silent, not daring to utter the first word. She would see what he wanted first, although she was sure she knew what he would say.

"You killed Noah," Vincent said, gesturing to Noah's body.

Ava hovered over Noah, sobbing inconsolably. Leah knelt next to her sister, attempting to comfort her by rubbing her shoulder and murmuring soothing words.

"Why did you do all this?" Vincent asked, his normally soft brown eyes hard. "Why did you bring us here, and why do you want us dead? You still haven't told us why you're torturing us. We deserve answers."

Camille laughed, and Brody hovered close to her. "I'm the writer, so I make the rules. In my books, I get to call the shots. I'm the one in control. I decide who lives and who dies. Manipulating situations and seeing how people react to them is great fun. Even when it was simply fiction, I had fun with it. But after I found this typewriter, the possibilities became endless. I can bring people to life and do with them whatever I please. It's my world. I can do anything. I can destroy anyone who gets in my way," Camille said, sounding drunk with power. "With my previous book, the characters didn't last nearly this long, so you should be proud of yourselves. They weren't as resourceful or clever. They didn't figure out what was going on and died much sooner than all of you."

"No one should have that kind of power," Vincent said solemnly, clutching the axe.

"You mean you've done this before?" Leah asked, her eyes turning away from her sister for a moment and sharpening in horror.

Camille cocked an eyebrow. "Of course. The first time was a trial, and I learned so much from it. The more practice I get, the better each book will be. This book will turn out even better than the last one. I bet my publisher is going to love it. Books are so much better when the characters come to life." Camille chuckled again. "*Literally.*"

"No one else knows about the typewriter?" Vincent gazed at the typewriter, stroking the dark stubble on his chin.

"No, no one except the old man who gave it to me. Why would I tell someone about it?" Camille clutched her charred sweater and her stomach as she willed her body to cooperate so she could stand.

"Not even your husband?" Vincent further questioned her, his eyes probing into her soul.

"He knows nothing," Camille said forcefully, gritting her teeth.

"Where is he really?" Vincent asked.

Camille's eyes narrowed, and she slowly stood. Vincent copied her and stood, so they were at eye level.

"I already told you. Japan."

"I don't believe you. In fact, I think almost everything you've told us is a lie. I don't trust you at all. How do I know you're telling the truth?" Vincent tossed the axe back and forth from hand to hand.

Camille's eyes remained glued to it as she wondered if she could take it from him forcefully, or if she should try to run.

"What do you mean?" Camille batted her eyes innocently, debating her next move.

"I haven't seen any signs of a man living here with you. So, either you aren't married and you made him up, or you're divorced and your husband hasn't been here in a while."

A smile flickered across Camille's face briefly before it vanished. She had to acknowledge his intelligence. It was the quality she was most attracted to. What a shame things hadn't turned out differently between them. "Clever. You're right."

"About what part?"

"Robert hasn't lived here in a while, so I got rid of most of his belongings. Some of his stuff is still in our main house. But you're wrong about one thing."

"What's that?" Vincent inquired.

"He never left." Camille stared out the window near her desk that overlooked the yard and her barren garden. "He's been out there all this time."

"Wh—what?" Vincent faltered, as if he couldn't believe what she was saying. Or he didn't want to.

Good. She caught him off guard when he thought he knew everything. No one likes a know-it-all.

Camille faced him dead-on and shook her head with regret. "You remind me of him too much, Vincent. I made a mistake in creating you. Next time, I'll make sure I don't create a character so similar to Robert. It's painful to see the younger version of him in the flesh—his clone. The way he looked back when he loved me and told me that we would be together forever. There's nothing like adolescent love to make you believe your life will be perfect, as long as you have each other. Oh, how wrong I was. You know, he built this cabin to be my writing retreat. He was so sweet in the beginning, always trying to do nice things for me and make me happy. I used to think he was supportive of my writing, but it was all a lie. I can't quite put my finger on what changed, but eventually, he became mean. Cruel. He didn't understand me, didn't understand my compulsion to write. He didn't like that I wasn't earning much money from my books, while I spent so much of my time writing them. Maybe he thought after so many years of publishing so many books we would be millionaires." Camille paused and chuckled ruefully. "Robert grew to resent me and complained every time I insisted that I needed to write. He always reminded me how hard he worked. He was always gone traveling for business. *An important businessman.*" She snorted derisively.

"I found out he was cheating on me with women in different cities all over the country. That was the real reason he traveled so often. To get away from me. But I was naïve. I thought I could get back what we had before, even after I found out about the cheating. I couldn't give up on my distorted vision of our marriage. I gave him another chance, and for a while, I thought things were better. Later on, he wasn't happy when he found out about the typewriter and what I was using it for. That was a mistake—telling him the truth. I thought he would understand. He was my true love, my Robert, so he should have understood why the typewriter was the perfect tool for me. I wish I had kept that secret to myself. But that doesn't matter now. Robert never left the cabin. He's been here with us this whole time. Even now, I can feel his presence. And you're all going to join him. There's plenty of room in the garden for a few more bodies."

Chapter 41: Leah

Leah's eyes darted around the cabin, searching for a weapon. They needed to get rid of Camille, or at least incapacitate her. Not only was she insane, she was dangerous. She had already killed one of them, so it was likely she wouldn't stop at just one.

Leah patted her sister on the back again, doing her best to soothe her. She could only imagine the grief she was grappling with. But they were in a life-or-death situation. Leah couldn't let herself think about the fact that Noah was dead, or she might fall apart too.

Vincent had the axe, but Camille was cunning. What if Camille took it from him or overpowered him somehow? Camille was clearly strong, mentally and physically. Leah couldn't let her get the upper hand. She needed to protect Vincent and Ava. She couldn't lose anyone else.

Leah made eye contact with Vincent, who smiled at her, his dazzling smile reserved just for her. Automatically, she smiled back, despite the fear rising in her as each second ticked by. He was hers, and no force on earth would tear them apart. Not even Camille and her magical typewriter.

As she contemplated what to do, Vincent charged toward Camille. He swung the axe wildly. Camille backed up and gripped the axe handle.

She halted it from coming any closer. A struggle for control of the axe ensued. Vincent and Camille each tugged on the handle. Leah watched the struggle, wanting to help Vincent. But she didn't want to get in the way or make things worse. She hadn't acted quickly enough. She only hoped Vincent would win the fight.

Vincent grunted as his grip loosened. Camille laughed victoriously, thinking she had won. Vincent doubled down on his efforts. He yanked the axe from Camille's hands. Then, swinging it back and then forward, he aimed for Camille's neck. He missed and chopped off her ear. The axe sliced through the creamy white flesh. A series of intense screams came from Camille.

"Vincent, help..." Camille said. Helplessly, she cupped her hand to her head. But it didn't stop the spurting blood from coming out. Brody yelped around her, distraught at the sounds of his owner's screams.

"Vince, no!" Leah yelled.

But it was too late. Vincent swung the axe toward Camille again. He chopped at the flesh of her neck as Camille continued to scream. Eventually, her screams weakened, then stopped altogether. Leah didn't think she would ever forget the sound of Camille's horrified, pain-filled screams as she fell to the floor. Brody's yelping intensified as he ran in frantic circles around the body of his former owner. Leah stared in horror at the sight of the still body. Blood dripped from Vincent, who stood panting next to the deceased writer.

What. The. Hell.

"Vince," Leah cried, tearing her gaze from Camille and turning to her boyfriend.

Tears streaked her cheeks, and she wiped them away, wondering why he had done it. What had gone through his mind? What came over him? And could she ever forgive him for killing someone? He had only done it to save her and Ava, right?

Vincent turned away from Camille's lifeless body to make eye contact with her. Sweat glistened on his face in the light of the fire. His chest heaved. He still held the blood-speckled axe in his hands. Leah bent down to pick up Brody, who was howling inconsolably after trying futilely to wake his owner by licking her face. *Poor dog.*

Leah went to the armchair and sat down with Brody in her lap. She stroked his soft fur and whispered to him, comforting both the dog and herself.

Ava had been silent throughout most of the ordeal. She approached Leah and stood next to her, then Ava wrapped her arm around Leah's shoulder and hugged her. Leah resumed her sobbing.

"We're okay. We're safe now," Ava promised, her voice soothing.

"No, that's not why I'm crying," Leah protested. "He—he killed her."

Vincent remained by Camille. He bent down to examine the body. Leah tore her eyes away again, not wanting to know what he was doing or what he was thinking.

Ava continued comforting Leah. Eventually, she calmed down a bit, enough to stop crying and attempt to think about what they should do next.

"We're still here," Leah realized with a start, the thought shattering through her mind like breaking glass.

The others looked at her.

Ava spoke first, "Does this mean we won't die, then? I thought maybe once Camille was gone..." She didn't finish the sentence, but they all knew what she meant.

Vincent agreed, "I thought so too, but I guess we're fine. What should we do with the body?" He glanced at Camille's corpse. "Should we bury her? What if someone comes by the cabin, like the police?"

Leah nodded as she held Brody in her arms, cuddling his small body. "Yeah, we can bury her in the garden. She has a shovel out there."

Leah walked to the window and looked out into the yard, surveying the empty garden. The grass was lifeless, with piles of old leaves scattered across the yard.

"The snow is gone," she said with wonder.

Ava joined her at the window, peering outside too. "Whoa. Not just gone, but like—"

"Like it never existed," Leah finished for her.

Ava shook her head. "Vincent, come on, help us with the body. We'll bring her outside, dig a hole in the garden, bury her, and then do one last sweep of the cabin before we leave."

Vincent didn't say anything at first. "I had to do it," he said firmly. "Camille was going to kill me, and she wouldn't stop until all of us were dead. There's no way she would have let us live. She killed her husband. She was deranged."

"We'll talk about it later," Leah said dismissively, not wanting to hear him talk that way.

She still wasn't sure Vincent had made the right decision. Plus, he had done it without consulting her. Had he even thought about how she would feel? Shivering and stepping further away from him, she rubbed her arms. She was dating a murderer.

"I had to do it," Vincent repeated.

"Let's go." Leah opened the front door.

A blast of sunlight shot through the cabin, illuminating the room and shattering the darkness they had become accustomed to.

Ava hesitated by the door. "We can't leave Noah like that," she said, her voice unnaturally soft. "We can't leave him here. Do you think we... Can we use the typewriter to bring him back?"

Chapter 42: Leah

Leah's eyebrows shot up in surprise. Why hadn't she thought of that? Perhaps because Noah was her sister's boyfriend, and Ava would do anything to save him.

"It's worth a shot," Leah responded, heading to the desk.

"I'm going outside," Vincent announced, hoisting up Camille's body into his arms and dragging it outside by himself.

Leah sat in the chair in front of the desk and placed her fingers on the keys of the typewriter. She looked at her twin with a quizzical expression. "What do I write? I can't just say, 'and then Noah came back to life,' can I? It's not like there's an instruction manual for this thing. We don't know how any of this works."

Ava's eyes filled with tears again. "Just type it. That's what I did for the front door lock and the windows. We have to try. It has to work." She gritted her teeth and peered over Leah's shoulder as she typed.

Once Camille was out of the cabin, Leah, Ava, Vincent, and Noah were safe. The axe hadn't pierced any of Noah's vital organs, and his bleeding stopped. He lay on the ground, then suddenly, he sat up, gasping for breath. He was alive.

Leah turned around to see her sister's reaction. "What do you think? Is it enough?"

"I'm not sure, but I hope so."

"Let's go see."

Leah and Ava walked hand in hand to Noah and waited for something to happen. Camille hadn't explained the details of how the typewriter worked. If they were only characters in her book and not real people, then couldn't they come back to life? It's not like they could really die. They would just vanish from the world, as if they had never existed outside of Camille's imagination.

Noah sat up, gasping for breath. He clutched his chest, where dried blood had crusted on his flannel shirt. He looked down at his chest, examining himself for injuries. Ava practically tackled him as she leaped into his arms and sprinkled his face with kisses.

Noah grunted from the pain and held Ava in his arms.

"I'm okay. Everything will be okay," he promised her.

***

Leah, Ava, and Noah joined Vincent outside. Vincent shoveled a few more piles of dirt on top of the mound in the garden, covering the body of the writer who had grappled with power, the blurred lines between fiction and reality, the writer's elusive, but constant struggle of trying to write the next Great American Novel, and the loneliness that invades the minds of so many. It was hard to believe that after everything they had been through over the past week, it was all over.

Vincent shoveled the last of the dirt onto the mound and patted the top down to smooth it out, spreading the dirt more evenly so the mound wasn't as obvious. Ava had crafted a little wooden cross out of some small twigs she had found in the woods nearby, and she placed it at the top of the grave.

The four of them gathered around the grave, heads bowed and hands clasped together, praying to whatever was out there listening that it was really over.

When they left the garden and went back into the cabin, Leah glanced back several times, half-expecting to see a hand claw its way out of the dirt and into the open air toward them *Carrie*-style, but no such thing happened.

Once inside, they solemnly gathered their things, grabbing extra supplies, food, and water from Camille's kitchen.

When Leah protested, Noah said, "What? It's not like she'll be needing any of this stuff."

He had a point.

Leah exited the cabin and stared back at it for a moment, as if in a daze. She closed her eyes, relishing the feeling of the sun beating down on her skin. The snow and cold seemed to be gone for good. The spring weather was officially here.

Vincent closed the door of the cabin and said, "Good riddance to this place. Let's get the hell out of here."

"What's going to happen to us?" Leah asked, anxiously glancing around the cabin, the woods, and toward the garden where they had buried Camille's body.

Noah shrugged. "Beats me. It seems like we're okay, though."

Ava agreed. She clapped a hand on Leah's shoulder. "Everything will be fine now. We'll go home and see Mom and Dad and—" She abruptly stopped talking, most likely realizing that there was no home. There was no Mom or Dad. They had nowhere to go and no one waiting for them or expecting them to return home. They didn't exist.

"I guess we'll figure it out?" Leah suggested, mimicking Noah's nonchalant shoulder shrug. "At least we have each other."

Leah grabbed Vincent's hand, wanting a steady force to hold on to.

They continued on, with Ava and Noah close behind them. When they reached the tree line at the edge of the woods, a tingling sensation spread through Leah's body. The tingling soon turned into a feeling akin to when her foot fell asleep, but throughout her entire body.

"Vince!" she exclaimed, looking down at her hand holding his.

Their hands were disappearing.

"Maybe we need to go back to the cabin. It could be something to do with being too far away from the typewriter," Vincent suggested in a panic. "Come on!" He started back toward the cabin, pulling Leah along with him.

Hastily, Vincent opened the front door and went inside the place they had been held captive. He and Leah strode over to Camille's desk, where the typewriter sat innocuously. It looked like a completely ordinary typewriter, making it difficult for Leah to believe it had once held so much power over them. Or that it still did if they couldn't leave the confines of the cabin for long.

What are we supposed to do?

Brody came running into the main room of the cabin from the hallway, barking up a storm at the intruders in his home. Leah gasped when she realized that in the craziness of killing Camille, getting rid of the body, and burying her, they had completely forgotten about the dog. She reached out her hand toward Brody and let him sniff her before she petted him.

Vincent shuffled through the papers on Camille's desk once again, rapidly flipping the pages over as he scanned for anything helpful. "This is hopeless! It's not like there's a guide to use this thing. We don't even know how it works." He pointed at the typewriter and then ran his hands through his messy ponytail.

Leah examined her hand, then flipped it over and looked at Vincent's as well. Their hands were completely solid again. No sign that they had been disintegrating.

Shit. Did that mean they were stuck in the cabin?

Leah contemplated the situation and thought about everything that had happened to them so far. "If Camille was controlling us with the typewriter and everything she wrote came true, maybe we can use the typewriter to our advantage. We used it to bring back Noah. Maybe we can use it to leave too. We can write something to help."

Vincent looked at her and then at the typewriter. "Hmm, maybe. What do you suggest?"

"I thought we could type something about us being real and getting home safely," Leah said.

Ava chimed in, "But what's the point of going anywhere if we don't really have a home? Why would we go all the way back to Michigan? It's not like we were ever there to begin with. It was all just part of our backstory as characters in Camille's book. We didn't exist in this world until a few days ago."

Noah nodded in agreement. "Yeah, we might as well stay in Asheville. Not in this cabin, obviously," he added. "But we could all get jobs and rent a place somewhere in the city."

"As long as it's not a cabin in the woods, then I'm down for that," Ava said, nodding along.

Leah stared at the typewriter, thinking. "I'm not sure if we can go more than a mile or two away, though. Remember the first time we tried leaving and how the van died? We ended up having to walk back here. And just now, we could barely leave the yard—"

"What if Camille's death somehow diminished where we can go?" Vincent said, stroking his chin thoughtfully.

"That's just great. So, we can't leave? What are we going to do?" Ava whined, flinging herself on to the couch dramatically.

Noah sat next to her and stroked her bleached-blonde hair.

Leah paced the room. Clearly, they couldn't stray too far from the cabin. It seemed like they either had to try writing something on the typewriter to help them and see if it came true, or they could accept their fates and stay in the cabin forever. But, Leah realized, there was a third option.

It didn't make sense if they couldn't wander away from the cabin. They had left before and made it miles away before they had been forced to come back. Leah assumed Camille had made them return to the cabin by adding something to her book about their van dying. It must have been Camille's interference with her writing that made them return.

The cabin had nothing to do with Camille's book or making her characters come to life. The power was all in the typewriter. That was what tied them here.

Leah puzzled over the last option, wondering if it was the best chance they had. It didn't seem like they had much of a choice.

They needed to destroy the typewriter.

Chapter 43: Leah

When Leah strode over to the typewriter, Vincent glanced up from his musings over Camille's files. The papers that held their words, their life stories, their heartaches, losses, grief, pain, and secrets within the ink. Camille had breathed their very essences into her words.

The typewriter was powerful. Much too powerful for anyone to own. Whoever had given it to Camille either hadn't known the power of it or they had been sadistic, wanting to unleash pain and suffering into the world.

"What are you doing?" Vincent barely had time to ask before Leah picked up the blood-soaked axe from where it was still laying on the ground in the spot where Camille had died.

Leah didn't answer him. She could make decisions without his input. Besides, he had done the same to her when he killed Camille. Breathing in deeply and bracing herself, she raised the axe above the typewriter, preparing to strike it down.

"Stop!" Vincent yelled, rushing toward her to intervene. "We don't know what the consequences of destroying the typewriter will be. We might disappear... for good."

Ava and Noah both stood from the couch and hurried to the desk.

Ava turned to her sister with a trusting expression on her face. "You have a reason for doing it, don't you, Leah?"

"Of course. I thought about every scenario. Destroying the typewriter is the best option we have," Leah responded. She elaborated on her thought process and how she had come to that conclusion and eliminated their other options.

"I think you're right," Noah said. "If we can't leave, then what's the point of living? At least if we destroy the typewriter, only two things can happen. Either it will work and we won't be tied to it anymore, and we'll be free to roam anywhere we want to. Or we're tied to the typewriter, and we can't exist without it. So, then—"

"Then we disappear," Vincent finished for him.

"Right," Leah agreed.

"Do it," Vincent said with a nod. "Destroy it."

Leah swung the axe in an upward motion, bringing it crashing down onto the typewriter. It glowed with power as she brought the axe down on it again, smashing into the cool, black metal and scattering the keys across the desk. The typewriter sparked. With one final swing, she slammed the axe into the typewriter again, hoping to eliminate the source of their suffering. The glowing intensified.

"Shit. What do we do with it?" Leah asked frantically, stepping back from it.

"Don't worry. I've got this," Vincent said. He ran into the kitchen, then quickly returned a minute later with potholders on each of his hands.

Noah burst out laughing, nearly doubled over. "Now isn't the time for cooking, Vincent," he rasped out in between laughs.

Vincent responded with an annoyed side-eye. He lifted the typewriter, grunting with the weight of it, and carried it over to the fireplace before realizing the fire had died. Smoke rose lazily from the remaining logs. "Fuck! Noah, start a fire!"

"Why are you—" Noah took in Vincent holding the glowing typewriter emitting sparks, then looked at the fireplace devoid of fire. "Oh... right."

Noah jogged to the fireplace and found the matches. He struck one across the matchbox. It failed to ignite. He struck a second match. The tiny flame sparked to life. He threw it into the fireplace. Rearranging the logs, he made sure several of them caught on fire before he stepped back and gestured for Vincent to go ahead.

Vincent hefted the typewriter into the air. They all watched as it soared into the fireplace, quickly catching on fire. Vincent backed up and yelled at Noah to do the same in case something happened. As Noah turned to back away from the growing fire, an explosion erupted. Several of the keys sprayed from the fireplace. The letter 'K' struck Noah and wedged itself into the skin of his throat. He grasped at the key and quickly yanked it out of his neck, which immediately spurted blood.

"Noah!" Ava screamed, moving forward.

Leah grabbed hold of her before she could go any closer to the fire.

"We have to get out of here," Leah insisted. "It's not safe. The entire cabin is going to go up in flames!"

"Noah!" Ava yelled again, shoving herself out of Leah's grip and darting toward her boyfriend.

"I'm fine." Noah gasped as blood sprayed from his neck.

He was losing blood much too fast. It seemed the key had struck an artery, so there was no way to stop the bleeding.

Vincent wrapped Noah's arm around his shoulders and started dragging him toward the front door. "Go! Get Ava out of here!" he yelled to Leah.

Leah hesitated for a few seconds before she obliged. She pulled Ava out of the cabin while she screamed and sobbed. Leah and Ava continued down the path toward the garden. When they reached the safety of the garden, Leah paused, looking back at the cabin. Why hadn't Vincent and

Noah caught up to them yet?

"Vince?" she shouted, not seeing her boyfriend. "Noah?"

Ava clung to her, desperately wringing her hands. "Where are they?" she sobbed.

"They're coming," Leah said unconvincingly.

Ava tried to run back to the cabin, but Leah held onto her firmly, not wanting her sister to be in danger.

"Come on, let's get a little further away, and we can wait for them," Leah said. "They'll be out soon. Noah is so frickin' muscular that it's probably a struggle for Vincent to help him get out," she said, attempting a weak joke.

Ava smiled, despite her tears and the dire situation. She squeezed Leah's hand, clutching it so tightly that Leah swore she heard the bones in her fingers crunching.

"They'll be out soon," Leah repeated, staring at the cabin, praying to God she was right and they hadn't just left their boyfriends to die.

Chapter 44: Leah

As Ava clutched her hand, Leah noticed both of their hands were disappearing as they had earlier. They were fading away. She shrieked and yanked Ava's hand away from hers, realizing too late that she was going to scare her sister when she should try to remain the calm, rational one. That was her role—she needed to be calm, for her sister's sake. It was already bad enough that Noah had died once; he might die again, and so might they.

Ava stared in disbelief at her hand when she looked down and saw the source of Leah's scream. "It's happening again!"

Leah stared at the cabin, willing Vincent and Noah to come outside. She wondered what was taking so long. They should have been out by now. Had the fire spread more and trapped them inside the cabin? Had something else happened? What if they were dead?

She glanced down to see that her hands were completely gone up to the wrist now. She wondered how much longer they had, and what they could do to stop themselves from disappearing.

"What should we do?" Ava asked, biting her lip and looking at her for answers as she usually did.

But Leah didn't have the answers this time. She had no clue what would become of them after they disappeared. If they were only characters in a book, then surely there wasn't a heaven or hell or any sort of afterlife in which they could exist? They would simply be gone, as if they had never been there. And no one would ever know what had happened to them since Camille was dead. The thought was chilling. Leah shivered, her teeth clashing together violently as she tried to fight off the encroaching coldness that had washed over her.

"I don't know," she finally whispered, so quietly she wondered if Ava had even heard her.

Ava bent her head down low, and her blonde hair fell forward, covering her face. She remained in that position for a few minutes until she looked up again. Fresh tears covered her cheeks. Leah wanted to reach out to comfort her, to hold her hand, hug her, or squeeze her shoulder in reassurance. But how could she do any of those things without hands?

Their arms were almost entirely gone now. Leah sat on the damp grass, not caring that the dew immediately soaked her pants. It's not like she would feel the wetness for long, so she wasn't worried about it. She tried to motion for Ava to sit next to her, but realized she couldn't.

"Sit next to me," Leah suggested. "We'll wait for them to come out."

Ava whimpered as she joined Leah on the ground and leaned against her. "What if they don't come out, and we never get to see them again?"

"They will be here soon."

"How do you know?"

"They wouldn't leave us alone," Leah insisted.

"Not on purpose," Ava replied, as more tears fell down her cheeks. Without hands or arms, she couldn't wipe them away, so the tears rolled down her face, splashing onto her sweater. "Should we go back in the cabin and make sure they're okay? What if something happened?"

"What would have happened? Camille is dead."

But part of Leah wondered if Ava was right. Why weren't they outside by now? What if Noah's injury had been worse than they thought?

Her feet and ankles were gone, and her legs were vanishing too. Leah tried to stand and found that she could float through the air, hovering above the ground slightly. She shook her head in disbelief. Why should she be shocked at being able to float? Nothing made sense anymore.

"Okay, maybe you're right. Let's go check on them," Leah said.

Ava watched Leah float and attempted to copy her. They floated unsteadily toward the cabin as they adjusted to their newfound power and hovered outside the front door, which still stood wide open.

"Vince?" Leah yelled, projecting her voice into the cabin.

"Noah!" Ava shouted even louder.

Leah entered the cabin first, drifting in and wildly glancing around inside, searching for Vincent and Noah. Upon scanning the main room, she saw Vincent bent over Noah, futilely trying to staunch the bleeding in his neck. He didn't have hands anymore either, so he was bent down on the ground, holding a rag to Noah's neck with his leg.

Ava began sobbing harder than ever when she saw Noah. His eyes were closed, but he briefly opened them when he heard Ava's cries.

"Ava..." Noah mumbled.

While Ava cried over Noah's body, Leah ran to Vincent. Their eyes met, and soon Leah's eyes glistened with tears.

"This is it," Leah told him. "It was all for nothing."

"It wasn't for nothing," Vincent said, stepping closer to her. "I love you."

"I love you too," Leah said.

Vincent leaned down to kiss her, but just as their lips were about to touch, he vanished. Leah screamed, but the scream seemed to catch in her throat as she vanished too.

The fire continued to burn in the fireplace, but the typewriter stood on the right side, wedged in between two logs, undamaged, as if the fire hadn't hurt it at all. In fact, the typewriter looked unscathed, minus the missing key for the letter 'K.' The typewriter was pristine and shiny, as if it was brand new.

Camille was buried in her garden. Leah and her friends were gone. But the typewriter lived on.

Epilogue

May 1988

Camille's eyes fluttered open. Soreness permeated throughout her entire body. As she attempted to stretch her aching body, she noticed someone sitting next to her. Confusion hit her as she tried to make sense of what had happened. Her memories were fuzzy, and she wasn't sure where she was.

She glanced to her right and saw spindly trees and mountain peaks fly by. She was in a car, she realized, and they were speeding down the winding highway at an impossible speed. How had she gotten here?

The man driving the car seemed familiar, with his twinkling blue eyes and cowboy hat, but she couldn't quite place him. Where did she know him from? She opened her mouth to speak, to ask who he was, but she couldn't form the words.

What was going on? Where was he taking her? Panic set in as the seriousness of the situation hit her. He could be dangerous, and she had no way of escaping unless she jumped out of the speeding car. That would surely lead to her death, so they drove on in silence.

Soon, the man stopped the car in front of a house that seemed to appear out of nowhere. Camille shook her head, dazed. There hadn't been a house there a few seconds ago.

A familiar sensation snuck over her, as if this had happened before. While Camille looked at the unremarkable house, a memory of the yard struck her. This was the house with the yard sale she had gone to months ago.

She peeked at the man again. He seemed different somehow, but he was the man who gave her the typewriter!

"Well, missus, are ya gonna get out of the car?" he asked with a broad smile. He stepped outside and shut the door.

Camille hastily opened her own door and exited the car, following him. She noticed the car was a sleek, brand-new, red Corvette convertible.

"How did you find me? Is this something to do with the typewriter?" she demanded. "Wait a second. I thought I was going to die. They were trying to kill me! Why am I still alive?"

The man removed his hat and grinned at her.

With a startle, Camille saw that the elderly man appeared younger now. His hair was less white and more of a dark brown. His wrinkles were gone, and his clothes looked freshly ironed.

"Did you enjoy the ride?" he asked with a sinister smile.

"Did you... Did you save me?" Camille asked him with wonder as she pondered the power of the typewriter.

He placed his hat securely back on his head. Then he reached out for her with his hand, and that's when Camille noticed the claws.

"I wouldn't quite call it salvation, hon."

Note from the Author

Hi Reader! Thank you so much for reading my latest thriller book. If you want to help me, I would appreciate it immensely if you wrote an honest review for *These Deadly Words*. Posting your review online is one of the best ways to support indie authors. Reviews help other readers decide which books they want to buy and allow indie authors to gain more exposure to new readers. Please consider posting a review on the book retailer website where you purchased the book and/or on Goodreads.

Acknowledgments

Being an indie author can be lonely at times, but I'm thankful to have so many supportive people in my life.

First and foremost, I want to thank my wonderful husband Zed. Not only does he put up with me constantly talking about the stories in my head, but he gives me feedback and helps me fix plot holes. He encourages me to keep writing, even when I'm stuck. Plus, he helps me at all of my book signings and always talks me up to potential readers. I couldn't do any of this without him.

My beta readers, Robert, Heather, and Evelyn, you all are amazing. They read an earlier draft of the book and spotted several issues that I was able to fix. They also let me know what parts of the book they loved, which is always encouraging while editing. I value my beta reader's input a lot, so I'm grateful to them for their assistance and constructive feedback.

I also want to mention one of my college professors, Michael Allen. In college, he let me take an independent study in playwriting, and he agreed to be my advisor. In that class, I wrote three plays. One of them was *The Hidden Story*, which *These Deadly Words* is based on. *The Hidden Story* won Adrian College's annual playwriting contest in 2014.

It was a huge part of what convinced me that being a writer was the right career choice. I can never thank Michael enough for believing in my writing talent and helping me find my voice.

I'm grateful to my amazing editors, BlackQuill Editing and Three Owls Editing, for making this book stronger. Thank you for pointing out inconsistencies, timeline issues, awkward wording, and typos. Publishing books is truly the work of many people besides just the author, and I couldn't do it without editors.

As always, thank you to my cover designer, Mandi Lynn of Stone Ridge Books. She always captures the very essence of my stories in her designs. I'm thankful to have her creative expertise for my books.

And last, but not least, to you—my readers. The ones who have been there since *The Long Shadow* series. The ones who anxiously wait for my next book. The ones who message me, email me, or comment on my posts. The ones who post book reviews, share my social media posts, tell your friends and family about my books, and help spread the word that my books are worth the read. The ones who just discovered my books. All of you. Thank you.

About Author

Nichole Heydenburg is the author of *These Deadly Words* and other thrillers for young adults, as well as *The Long Shadow* thriller trilogy for adults. She also owns Poisoned Ink Press, where she provides editing services to authors. She earned her Bachelor's Degree in English with an emphasis in writing from Adrian College. When she isn't writing, Nichole enjoys exploring new cities with her husband, reading, and drinking iced mochas. She currently resides near Asheville, NC with her husband Zed and their crazy rescue dog, Mr. B.

Subscribe

If you're interested in being a part of the first group of readers to learn about:

- My upcoming book releases and works in progress

- Cover reveals and ARCs

- Exclusive book content

- Book sales and freebies

- Giveaways

- In-person book events

Sign up for my newsletter on **www.nicholeheydenburg.com**!

9 781734 901597